Give a Man
a Gun

Give a Man a Gun

John Creasey

PERENNIAL LIBRARY

Harper & Row, Publishers, New York
Cambridge, Philadelphia, San Francisco, Washington
London, Mexico City, São Paulo, Singapore, Sydney

A hardcover edition of this book was originally published in England under the title *A Gun for Inspector West*. A hardcover edition of *Give a Man a Gun* was published in the United States in 1954 by Harper & Brothers.

First PERENNIAL LIBRARY edition published 1987.

Library of Congress Cataloging-in-Publication Data
Creasey, John.
   Give a man a gun.
   Previously published as: A gun for Inspector West. 1. Title.
PR6005.R517G8   1987   823'.912   87-45038
ISBN 0-06-080886-1 (pbk.)

87 88 89 90 91 OPM 10 9 8 7 6 5 4 3 2 1

Give a Man
a Gun

1

The Chase

"Has he a gun?" asked West.

"Not sure, sir," the sergeant behind him said.

"Well, be careful."

"Yes, sir."

The voices whispered in the darkness. The two men—West of Scotland Yard and a uniformed sergeant—were together at one end of an alley which ran between two warehouses. High brick walls were on either side, cobbles underfoot. At the far end, the water of the Thames lapped against wharves, small boats and an ocean-going cargo vessel registered at Rotterdam.

There should have been a light along there, fastened to a wall bracket. Instead, there was darkness.

More policemen were going a long way round toward the river, hoping to cut off the fugitive they knew to be near. At this end, coming from the mean streets of the East End toward the docks, were West and his sergeant; detective officers in plain clothes were just behind them.

The hunted man was in the alley, perhaps armed with a gun.

West, a yard ahead of the others, put his foot in a puddle. The splash sounded very loud. West stood stock still, and the sergeant bumped into him.

West went forward again, very cautiously. The lapping waves of the Thames seemed part of the silence. Above, heavy clouds scudded, but there was no wind here. No stars shone. The docks were deserted but for a few night watchmen.

A killer had come along this lane, and the killer had to be captured.

West could hear the sergeant's labored breathing; fancied that he could hear the movement of two constables behind them. Like the lapping waves, they seemed part of the hush. West's heart beat fast; the unknown darkness was a frightening thing.

Dark silence....

Noise smashed it. A clatter, a crash, then the footsteps of a man running.

"Careful!" gasped the sergeant.

West's torch stabbed its light along the alley. It fell on a man running toward him, only thirty yards away. The glare made the man's eyes shine as if they were light themselves; it showed his open mouth and pounding legs and swinging arms —and the knife in his right hand. The blade shimmered, like silver.

"Your torch!" rasped West.

"Be careful!"

"Switch on!"

The footsteps pounded, the glittering eyes looked baleful, the right hand with the knife in it grew steadier; the man raised his arm, as if to throw the knife. The sergeant's torch flashed out. The fugitive was only thirty yards away from West now, and the passage echoed to the thud of his footsteps.

"Stop there!" West called. "You haven't a chance. Stop there!"

The man pounded on.

"Careful, sir!"

"It's all right," West said, as if there were no urgency.

He moved his torch. The running man saw the snaking beam, and was bewildered for the moment that mattered. The light shone on the shimmering blade. The knife was held to cut or stab, not to throw, and the man was only fifteen yards away from the police.

He ducked beneath the torch. It flew over his head and clattered on the cobbles behind him; the light went out, but others flashed on.

West started moving as he threw the torch, raced forward, and was on the man before he recovered from the moment of surprise. They reeled under the shock of the collision, then West thrust his left arm upward, groping for the other's right wrist. He felt a sharp blade across the back of his hand, but gripped the wrist and twisted.

"Oh!"

It was a gasp, a squeal of pain. The man's fingers went dead, and the knife dropped and clattered. West, keeping his hold on the bony wrist, felt a knee driving up toward his groin, twisted the wrist again and brought another yelp. The knee brushed against West's hip.

Then the sergeant and others behind him drew level.

"Okay, sir," the sergeant said breathlessly. Torch-

3

light fell onto the pale, youthful face and the thin fingers. The steel of handcuffs glinted, there was a sharp click. "That's got him, sir."

"Fine," said West. "Be careful with that knife, there might be some prints on it apart from his." He studied the young prisoner's thin face and quivering lips. "One of you go and pick up my torch, will you? What have you been up to?" he added in the same casual voice to the prisoner. "You're old enough to know you can't go round cutting people up."

The prisoner didn't speak; his breathing was harsh and labored with fear.

"Come on, talk," West said. "We won't eat you. Why did you do it? What had Old Benny done to you?"

Words came out in a gust.

"I hate his guts!"

"And you put a knife in them," West said. The difficulty was to keep his voice casual, not to let the youth know what he felt; not to let his men realize that he could have smashed the pale face to pulp, because of what the youth had done to an old man. "How did it start? What happened?"

"You won't make *me* talk."

West had been hopeful of getting a statement; the voice and manner dashed all hope. He stopped trying.

It was cold. Police cars were gathered in a nearby street, and the officers who had been sent to cut off the fugitive were streaming into the alley, from the far end.

"Take him away," West said.

"Yes, sir—here's your torch. Bulb's gone, I'm afraid."

4

West took it. "Thanks."

Soon they were in a lighted street, with little houses on one side and warehouse walls on the other. Headlights from several police cars made the street lamps seem dim. The prisoner was hustled into a car and driven off, still handcuffed. Police from the Divisional Headquarters stood about, waiting for a move from West of the Yard.

A Yard sergeant, Peel, had been on the wharves. He came hurrying.

"You all right, sir?"

"Yes, Jim, thanks. We'll go and see Old Benny again, I think." West turned to his car. "You drive." He flashed a smile to the Divisional men. "I don't need to tell you chaps what to do. Thanks for everything, and I'm glad we got him so quickly."

That was the kind of thing that warmed men in the Divisions to West of the Yard. They hovered about him as he climbed into his car, next to Peel, and watched as he was driven off.

West lit a cigarette and drew at it, closing his eyes and seeing vivid mental pictures.

They weren't nice.

Old Benny had been badly cut up. He had been a rogue, but in his way an attractive rogue. He had been in prison three times, and until that night could always smile and be amiable with the police, being free from all bitterness. Crime had been his livelihood, the police his natural enemies. At seventy, he had hoped to die out of prison.

Well, he had.

His niece had called the police. West was wondering about her. She was a pretty little thing, he knew, but much more bitter than her Uncle Benny had ever been. A dark-haired, bright-eyed rebel, which was a pity. She had known who was with her uncle in his bedroom when he had called out in alarm, had dialed 999, then rushed to the bedroom. But the killer, little more than a boy, had locked the door and escaped through a window.

It had happened an hour ago.

Luck, if it were luck, had taken West and Detective Sergeant Peel to the Divisional Headquarters that night, over inquiries about a forgery case. West had forgotten the forgery as soon as he heard of the murder of Old Benny.

Peel swung the car through the mean, narrow streets dotted with occasional lamps. It was nearly midnight. The East End looked asleep, whether it was or not. Soon they were in the wide Mile End Road, a drab main artery of London feeding the great mass of the East End.

Three cars were parked outside Old Benny's shop. There Benny had dealt in secondhand silverware, cutlery and jewels—anything which could be turned into easy money.

Lights streamed out from the windows, a few people hung about the pavement, furtive, curious.

Just inside the shop, talking to Old Benny's niece, was a tall, hook-nosed man, with heavy-lidded, very bright eyes.

"There's Brammer, the *Courier*'s bright boy," Peel said. "He didn't lose much time."

"No, he certainly didn't," agreed West. "Just stand by, Jim, will you?"

He was brusque; and Peel knew that it was because he was remembering Old Benny's wounds. He pushed his way through the little crowd, was recognized by a policeman at the door, and admitted with Peel on his heels.

"Hallo, Handsome." Brammer's smile was just a sardonic curve of thick lips.

"They shouldn't have let you in," West said, but forced himself to look amiable. "Don't use anything until we've had a minute together, will you?"

He turned to Ruth Linder.

Hostility showed in her eyes, but was less marked than usual because shock was also there. She hadn't lost her color. She wasn't just a pretty little thing, she was a beauty. Her hair had the dark gloss of a raven's wing, and she had that perfect complexion, slightly sallow, which some Jews and many Spaniards and Italians have when they are young.

"I shouldn't talk much to the Press, Miss Linder."

She didn't answer.

"Come with me, will you?"

West turned, and the girl followed. He knew that she was glowering at his back. It was not a good feeling. He was aware of no reason why she should hate the police, but the hatred was there, and it might make her a difficult witness.

The parlor, at the back of the shop, was crowded with police.

"Let's go upstairs," West said to Ruth Linder, and led the way again.

The staircase was narrow, the carpeted boards creaked. There were only two rooms on the next floor—a sitting room on the right, the old man's bedroom on the left. Lights were on in both.

West knew that the police surgeon and others would be with Old Benny, and didn't want to interfere with them. He put his head inside the room, and said:

7

"I'm back."

"Okay," grunted a man who was bending over the bed.

West could see red stains on the sheet; there was even a red splash on the wall of the small room.

"Let's go to the other room," West said to the girl.

Her bedroom, he knew, was on the floor above. The room they entered now was a combination of stock room, office and sitting room. A big, old roll-top desk was in one corner, with a bright light shining above it. Shelves round the walls were littered with oddments from books to silver plate, trays of cheap jewelry to odd pieces of china. Easy chairs were in front of a fireplace.

"Sit down," West said.

"I prefer to stand."

Her speaking voice was excellent, there was no trace of the lisp her uncle had never been able to cure in himself.

"Please yourself," West said. "I'm going to sit." He dropped into an old saddlebacked armchair, which he knew that Old Benny had kept for guests. Murderers and thieves as well as policemen sat in that chair over the years. "Listen," West went on; "this is one of the things you can't blame us for."

She didn't answer, so he went on:

"You said before that you heard them quarreling, because—"

"You just can't tell the truth, can you?" the girl said, in a taut voice. "It isn't even your fault; you just can't get things straight. I didn't say they were quarreling. I said I heard Neil Harrock shouting at my uncle. Uncle didn't shout back at him. It takes two to make a quarrel."

8

"All right," said West. "You heard Neil Harrock complaining that your uncle had cheated him by not paying enough for the jewels that Harrock had stolen. Is that right?"

"It can't do my uncle any harm now," Ruth Linder said. "Yes."

"You knew all about the deal they made, didn't you?"

"Not until I heard Harrock shouting."

West said slowly, "All right, I'll pretend to believe that you didn't know it. Listen to me, Ruth. Your uncle had a kink which turned him into a criminal. He was a generous, likable man, but he was always frightened of the police because—"

"Don't be a fool," she sneered. "The police couldn't *frighten* him, any more than they can me. They hounded him, but he was always fooling them. Don't kid yourself."

West took out cigarettes. She ignored the packet he held out. He lit up, watching her all the time. She tried to hold the sneer, but it wasn't easy because she was genuinely stricken with grief. She was very lovely, and she might go far—but there was some quality in her which would lead to ruin if she were not very careful.

"Ruth," West said, "you've had a bad shock. I'm sorry. I don't want to make the situation any worse. But you've got to get certain things straight. Your uncle first went to jail forty-four years ago. It was his own fault. He spent nineteen of the past forty-four years in prison. That means he wasted nineteen years. That was his fault, too. Now he's dead, and you'll inherit a sizable fortune. You probably think that by serving his sentences he gave himself the right to the money he made.

9

Certainly you don't have to have his fortune on your conscience. But be satisfied with the money. Don't try to run the business, too. Don't buy and sell stolen goods. If you do, you'll soon learn all about prison."

"I know I'll have to make a statement about Neil Harrock," Ruth said, "but I don't *have* to listen to this drivel."

2

The Sentence

Five weeks later she gave evidence against Neil
Harrock at the Old Bailey. She gave it well, but
obviously held bitterness on a tight rein. She
looked superb in a mink coat, a tight little black
hat, and with diamonds scintillating on her hands.

West listened to her, worriedly.

He could not understand the underlying cause of
her bitterness, and it made him wonder whether
he was hearing the truth. Nothing in the investigation suggested that he wasn't. Harrock, a youngster of twenty-two, had said practically nothing,
but his fingerprints had been at the shop and on
the knife, together with blood from the same group
as the murdered man's.

Undoubtedly, Harrock had killed Old Benny.

All the pleading, all the tears of a distracted
mother, all the distress of a shocked father,
couldn't alter that fact.

West was glad that the parents weren't in court.

It would be a quick trial, and he doubted
whether it would run into a second day. Apart

11

from the police, Ruth Linder was the chief witness. Harrock had practically no defense.

He had been terrified and almost hysterical on the night of his capture, but was calmer now. It was possible to feel the stirring of admiration for him. Well-dressed, nice-looking, he showed no sign of fear. The Prosecution had to prove that he had stolen jewels from the shop where he worked; and did so, without trouble. The jewels had been found at Old Benny's. The case built up remorselessly, and the youth hardly flickered an eyelid.

When Ruth Linder was giving evidence, Harrock watched her closely, but showed no sign of resentment. Now and again he actually smiled at her faintly. It was almost as if he saw her beauty rather than heard her husky voice damning him.

The jury was out for only fifteen minutes; and the judge put on the black cap before he passed sentence.

Young Neil Harrock didn't flinch.

Roger West left the Old Bailey soon after the trial, and wasn't surprised when several newspapermen approached him. Brammer, actually a private investigator now attached to the *Courier*, was among them, still giving an apology of a smile, sardonic, almost arrogant. He stayed behind when all the others had gone.

Strictly speaking, Brammer wasn't a journalist. For years he had run his private inquiry agency, venturing far beyond the usual divorce and civil inquiries. A year before, the *Courier*—which had a three million circulation—had hired him to track down a runaway atom scientist. He had found the man in Italy.

12

Still officially a "private eye," Brammer now worked exclusively for the *Courier*, and his office was in the same Fleet Street building in the newspaper. Twice in the past year he had carried out "private investigations" into the causes of crimes with violence, and the *Courier* had published the results. In a way, Brammer was a spearhead for many *Courier* thrusts against what it called laggard authority. The newspaper took its duty to the public very seriously.

Brammer had never set out to annoy or run counter to the police.

"Another feather in your cap, Handsome," he said.

"That's right," Roger said. "You ought to tell the *Courier*'s bloodthirsty readers that I get a sadistic satisfaction out of sending kids to the condemned cell. They'll believe it."

"Troubled about this case?" asked Brammer. "Don't you think he did it?"

"I know he did it."

Brammer grinned crookedly.

"So you're worried about the chief witness, are you? I suppose you know that she hates the sight of you."

West said, "Do you meant that—of me?"

"Only as typifying all policemen."

"I tried to make her see sense." Roger offered cigarettes. They were in Ludgate Hill, on their own, and he led the way to the Circus and then into a café. He could have done with a drink, but it was too early. The café was almost deserted in the middle of the afternoon. "What do you know about her, Bram?"

"She just hates all policemen."

13

"Do you know why she should?" Roger was drawing very hard at his cigarette. "She doesn't seem to have any reason except that her uncle spent so much time in jail. I can't find out that she's got any personal motive."

"You haven't gone back far enough in her history," Brammer said. "I'm making a present of this to you, Handsome, because I can see she worries you. She'd be a nice girl if it weren't for this! She's the daughter of a man who was hanged for murder. Her mother committed suicide after the hanging. Old Benny adopted her, so to speak. Her real name is Lindermann, and you'll find everything in the records of fifteen years ago."

"How did you get hold of this?" asked Roger slowly.

"It was one of the first cases I ever covered for a newspaper," Brammer said. "I was very enthusiastic then, and after the human-interest angle—the child was all of that. You weren't out of the puppy stage, were you?" He gave his slow, sly grin. "Have another cuppa."

"Thanks," said Roger. "I'll check that story."

"It's gospel truth," Brammer assured him. "Would I lie?"

At the Yard, it took Roger twenty minutes to turn up the case history of the Lindermann trial. Everything that Brammer had said was there, except that no one was named as adopting the child.

There was other background information, too. The Lindermanns were Germans who had come to England as refugees. They hadn't been in London long before Lindermann had killed a woman, afterward proved to have been his mistress—an unpleasant, sordid business.

14

Brammer, a free-lance journalist in those days, had been prominent in it; there were press cuttings about stories he'd written up for a Sunday newspaper.

Roger telephoned the Division; several hours afterward Division called him back to say that one of the sergeants, near retiring age, remembered that Old Benny Kramer, a distant relative of the Lindermanns', had taken the girl in after the Lindermann case. There could now be no reasonable doubt as to the cause of Ruth's bitterness.

Yet West was still uneasy, and not sure that he knew all the truth about what had happened when Old Benny had been murdered. But he wouldn't listen when Peel suggested that the girl might have killed the old man, and that Neil Harrock was taking the rap.

"She may have put him up to it, and then ratted on him, but I can't see any possible reason why," Roger said. "There's no evidence that they knew each other before. Let's forget it."

He couldn't forget.

He twice saw Neil Harrock in the condemned cell, but the youth wouldn't talk about the case, seemed indifferent to the coming hanging, and said nothing to suggest that Roger did not know everything that had taken place in the shop in the Mile End Road.

Plenty happened to keep Roger's mind occupied. The graph of crimes of violence showed a sudden upward slant. A wave of coshing, knifing and shooting swept upon London. At one time Roger found himself with three murders and two attempted murders going through his hands at the same time—all involving youths in the late teens

15

or early twenties. The Press, led by the *Courier*, raised the familiar cry of "flog the brutes," and a wave of agitation for more severe penalties swept over the country after a policeman was shot and badly wounded in North London.

Yet day in and day out Roger found himself thinking about Ruth Linder and her bitterness.

Whenever he was in the Mile End Division he asked how things were going at the shop, which she ran with the help of a youthful assistant, Sol Klein.

There was nothing to suggest that she was receiving. The shop's legitimate trade seemed to be flourishing—perhaps because of Old Benny's death and sympathy for Ruth. She had inherited over fifty thousand pounds as well as the business. Soon she began to dress much more stylishly than she had ever done before. She had no regular boy friend, but was often out with different men. She spent more and more evenings in the West End, too.

"All the fellows she goes with are youngsters," Roger's informant told him, "about the same age as young Harrock."

"She isn't exactly an old hag herself, is she?"

"Twenty-six," he was told.

Obviously the different boy friends could be thieves; Ruth could be carrying on the dead man's business away from the shop; but there was no evidence to say so.

The first time Roger saw her, after the day in court, was by accident. She was getting out of a luxurious car at the Majestic Hotel, and he had been there about a light-fingered waiter. A remarkably handsome, youthful man was helping Ruth out. Roger knew the man by sight, but couldn't place him.

Roger stood in the hall, and watched.

Ruth didn't notice him until they were almost level. Then he saw her lips tighten, and she tossed her head as she went by. She didn't look round.

Her escort was obviously staying at the hotel, for he led the way to the lift and they were taken upstairs.

West went across to the reception desk.

"Who was that man? Do you know?"

"That was Sir Neville Hann-Gorlay," the clerk told him, "Member of Parliament for the Trend Division."

"Oh, yes, of course. And the girl?"

"Just a friend, I presume." The clerk kept a poker face.

As he drove away from the hotel, Roger kept seeing Ruth's face in his mind's eye. Hatred had glowed in her eyes, and her beauty, her obvious vitality, made the hatred an ugly thing.

Roger made a few inquiries into Hann-Gorlay's background. In his early thirties, the M.P. was well known for championing lost causes. Once or twice he had advocated much harsher measures with criminals who used violence. His independent attitude often brought him headlines and a clash with his party leaders. He was known to be extremely wealthy, was popular with everyone who knew him and had a brilliant military record.

In the next few weeks Hann-Gorlay was often seen with Ruth in the West End. She spent a week end in Trend. Soon afterward she moved out of the flat above the shop in the Mile End Road into a luxurious apartment in a block of flats near Park Lane.

Sol Klein was now in sole charge of the East End shop; but Ruth remained the owner.

The next thing which made Roger think of Old Benny's niece happened a month later. It was some time before he realized that it might involve her. During those hours the Yard reached a new high pitch of feverish energy. It was already at tension, for in the past four weeks several policemen had been attacked, while investigating something on their beat which seemed suspicious. But none had died.

P. C. Allenby of H Division was walking along Putney High Street, watching the dawn. His thoughts were hardly poetic, although it was a beautiful morning: cirrus clouds in miraculous array were gilded by the rising sun, and the sky was a strangely glowing blue. It was very cold and very late; on any weekday morning Putney would have been awake. This being Sunday, few people were about—only the milkmen, the newspaper boys and the police, like P. C. Allenby.

He was on his way to his station and breakfast, and was so hungry that he almost forgot that he was also very tired.

Glancing up because he saw a movement which subconsciously caught his attention, he saw a man on the roof of a bank.

It happened just like that. One moment there was the beautiful sky, empty rooftops and drab buildings; the next the man's figure appeared angled against the sky.

P. C. Allenby stared.

The man—he looked very young—disappeared.

18

Allenby snatched his whistle out of his pocket, blew vigorously and rushed across the road. He knew the bank and the fire escape which led to the back of it. He knew that the man on the roof would only escape easily that way. His feet thudded on the pavement. His whistle shrilled out again, and two newspaper boys and a busman, all cycling, pedaled more furiously toward him.

He swung round the corner, and saw the man, halfway down the fire escape.

Already rather breathless, he didn't blow the whistle again, but raised his fists, and called:

"Stop there!"

None of the three cyclists had reached the corner. The man was rushing down the staircase, which clattered and boomed. Allenby reached the foot of it.

"Take it easy, now." He was gasping for breath. "Don't you try—"

Then he stopped; and he knew what terror was.

The youth—he *was* very young—drew a gun.

Allenby put the whistle to his lips again and blew, but didn't give ground. He thought he heard one of the cyclists turn the corner. He certainly heard a shout.

"Put that gun away," he said breathlessly, "and—"

He didn't get a chance to finish.

The youth shot him, and the bullet caught him between the eyes.

The youth jumped to the pavement. A cyclist shouted. The youth turned round and fired at the cyclist; it was sheer luck that he caught the narrow tire. The cyclist felt the handlebars twist out his hand, and went flying over them. The youth

19

turned and ran along the street. Seeing what had happened to the first, the other cyclists slowed down.

They could see blood flowing sluggishly from P. C. Allenby's face.

It gave them a strange, creepy feeling, and was touched with unreality. They knew Allenby; they had never seen him lying down before.

The killer youth reached the corner and was round it before one of the newspaper boys made a queer noise in his throat, and said:

"We ought—we ought to chase—"

Then a car turned into the street, and slowed down. A policeman appeared, running. Confusion, bad from the start, became worse with every second. The killer escaped. The local police station was advised, and soon the news reached Scotland Yard.

It was Roger West's week end on duty.

He felt the sudden tension as the Yard geared itself to a tremendous effort.

3

High Pressure

Roger was at the Putney bank within forty minutes of the shooting. A crowd watched him walk with Detective Sergeant Peel toward the foot of the fire escape. Peel was big and boyish-looking, with a red, scrubbed face and fair hair. He moved his powerful body with superb ease. Roger, slightly shorter, although a full six feet, had features which justified his nickname—Handsome. He was brisk-moving and alert, and his gray trilby hat was tipped to the side of his head.

Putney detectives were waiting for him at the top of the fire escape.

"Can't find a thing," the inspector in charge said. He was a heavy-featured, bright-eyed man dressed in brown. "The swine got in through the roof light. Went down two flights of stairs, then came up against the steel door of the bank. He blew that, and—"

"Blew it?" asked West, sharply.

"Used something pretty powerful, too," the Putney man said. "After that, he blew the strong room.

21

Must have been crazy; he doesn't seem to have taken much."

"Who said so?" asked Roger.

"The manager's down there now," the Putney man told him. "He lives only a few doors along."

They went down through the roof light, then into the offices of a firm of accountants and next the offices of an estate agency. On the next staircase was a rubble of dust and debris.

"It must have made a hell of a noise," Roger said.

"There aren't many people living near here," the Putney man remarked.

A powerful explosive, probably nitroglycerine, had been used to blow the door of the bank and of the strong room. There was plenty of debris, and Putney police were going through it. Two safes had also been blown. The manager and a clerk, who lived nearby, were checking the contents of these. The manager, gray-haired and slow-moving, looked as if nothing would ever make him hurry.

"Glad to meet you, Chief Inspector." He gave a tired smile. "Not exactly what I like to do on Sunday morning!"

"No. Are you sure there isn't much missing?"

"Perhaps a thousand pounds."

"So you call that chicken feed?"

The old man looked mildly into Roger's eyes.

"He could have taken fifty thousand. He took only the old notes, which can't be traced, Chief Inspector."

"No fool, then," Roger said. "How long will it take you to prepare a complete list of what's missing?"

"It shouldn't take more than two or three hours,"

the bank manager said. His eyes twinkled. "That's if we don't have too many interruptions."

"I'll take your hint," Roger said, smiled, and left him.

The other police were already busy with routine. Roger watched, moving around and saying little. Footprints in the dust promised a clue, but there was no trace of fingerprints on top of the dust which the explosions had caused, so the solitary thief had used gloves or had plaster on his finger tips.

Then West saw several red, shiny spots in a corner, behind one of the strong room safes. He knelt beside it; the surface was coating over slightly, and the red was turning brown.

Others hurried across to him.

"The thief hurt himself badly," Roger said, pointing to smears on the cement floor. "See where he trod on the blood, while he stood here?" Shining a torch downward, Roger could see the tacky coating of blood. "It looks as if he bled freely, too. Now we can move—your book ready, Peel?"

"Ready, sir!"

"Get this call out to all London Divisions and Home Counties, special attention for neighboring districts to Putney. Man with badly wounded hand—"

"Hand?" Peel questioned.

"I can't see that any other part of him would bleed enough to drip like this—his clothes would soak the blood up," West explained. "Still, amend to 'probably hand.' Soles of boots or shoes, probably of rubber, may have traces of dried blood. Edges of the soles and heels ditto. Man probably under twenty-five, dark-haired—but you've got the description," Roger added. "Rush it, Jim."

"I'll radio at once," Peel said, and hurried into the street.

"Now we've got something," said the bulky Putney chief. "There weren't many people about this morning. I may get some word in from a patrol or from inquiries. I didn't lose *much* time."

"Of course you didn't," Roger said. He was staring at one of the open safes. "No sign of blood on that—anything on the other?"

They looked.

"No."

"So he bandaged himself up, or I'm wrong about the hand," Roger said. "Mind taking me along the road where the killer went?"

"Glad to."

"Mr. West," called the manager, unexpectedly.

"Hallo?"

"This makes it look as if you were right about the hand."

The manager held up two account books; the edges of the leaves were smeared with blood, and there was a tacky mess on the wine-red cover of one.

"Fine," Roger said, after examining it. "You took the wrong job!" The bank manager's twinkle grew more pronounced. "Thanks very much—test for prints right away," he added to a Yard man nearby, then led the way out into the street.

It was warm now; there wasn't a cloud in the sky. The crowd had grown to a hundred strong, and people were sauntering from each end of the road to increase it.

24

Policemen had roped off the spot where P. C. Allenby had fallen, but his body had been moved.

"According to the cyclists who saw it happen, he went up this way," the Putney man said.

"Been along here yourself yet?" Roger asked.

"Not yet; I couldn't see any need to."

"No," said Roger, absently. He moved toward Peel, who was sitting in a police car with a radio telephone in his hand. Peel kept on talking into it. "Which side of the road?" asked Roger.

"Well—"

"This side, most of the way; he crossed up there." A boy standing nearby pointed eagerly. "I didn't see him, but Jim Tee said he did. Jim's delivering his papers now, sir. Are you—*are* you Handsome West?"

"Idiots to call me that, aren't they?" West smiled. "Walk along the way this chap went, will you? Slowly, mind. See if you can see anything red and wet on the pavement."

"Who, *me?*"

"Why should I do all the work?" Roger smiled at him again. "It might look brown and tacky."

The boy hurried along, looking down at the ground. The Putney policeman obviously couldn't make up his mind whether he approved or not.

Peel finished, and came hurrying.

"Have 'em send a bloodhound here," Roger said. "Rush it. We might get that blood trail if we hurry."

"Right." Peel ducked back into the car.

The boy was walking ahead, with three others, all talking eagerly. His head was bent; he could not have scanned the ground more closely had he hoped to find a fortune. The other boys did the same. One suddenly dropped down on his knees, and began to crawl along, sniffing the ground.

Roger had to chuckle.

'You know, West, even if there is a trail it will be covered by this crowd walking over it." The Putney man could no longer keep his disapproval out of his voice. He glanced round at the crowd on their heels. "And it's hardly a joking matter."

Roger shot him a glance which was suddenly frosty.

"Isn't it?" he said. "Perhaps it's a laughing matter that you—" He broke off.

The other flushed.

"What were you going to say, Chief Inspector?" His voice was stiff, hostile.

"Forget it," Roger said shortly.

"What's *this?*" yelled one of the lads.

He was a few yards ahead of his fellows, and crouching low by the curb. The crowd behind surged forward. Police ahead of them threw a protective cordon quickly. In a moment, the boys, Roger and the Putney man in charge were ringed by police, and the police were ringed round by spectators, mostly men.

The boy was pointing to a brownish stain on the gray stone of the curb. Roger went down on one knee and touched it gently with a forefinger. He broke the surface; blood glistened beneath it.

"Nice work, son," he said warmly. "So our killer was crossing the road. See what you can find over there."

"Okay!" Eager lads forced their way through the two cordons.

"It looks as if he'd been holding his hand up, or perhaps had his hand in his pocket, and blood

26

gathered in a pool," Roger said. "Then a lot splashed down at once. Our good luck."

Almost opposite the spot where the boy had found the blood was an alleyway leading to the Thames. Beyond the end of the lane, the river flowed gently, the surface sparkling. The boys were already at the far end. Roger and the Putney man led the rest of the procession to join them.

They reached the wide road beyond the alley.

The boys were now standing at railings which protected the pavement from the river itself, pointing and talking excitedly. There was a small landing stage, where pleasure boats loaded and unloaded passengers.

"Any luck?" Roger asked the boys.

"Looks like it, Guv. See!" One of them pointed to brownish smears on the top rail, just above steps leading down to the landing stage. "Ain't *that* blood?"

Roger stared, and went closer....

"Yes, it is. Now we want someone who saw our man go off in a boat, Symes. Will you get cracking?"

Whatever the Putney man felt, he didn't hesitate.

"Right away," he promised briskly.

"Anything more we can do, Guv?" asked the boy who had first spoken to Roger.

"Give me your names and addresses," Roger said. "And that's about the lot."

They began to scribble....

A man who had been fishing on the river bank, a hundred yards along, had seen a youth leave the landing stage in a small motorboat.

Roger promptly started things moving along the river.

River police and riverside patrols were called to the hunt. Hundreds of police began to question thousands of people. The motorboat was trailed farther downriver, to Wandsworth Bridge, then Battersea, then Albert. It took time, but the reports were clear-cut; there was no doubt that it was the same motorboat.

A description of the youth in it was quickly built up.

Dark hair, sallow-faced, wearing a brown coat and flannel trousers, with leather patches at the elbows of the jacket. A lock of hair falling over his forehead. He needed a haircut. He needed a shave. He kept his left arm bent and pressed against his chest. He had a thick bandage of some kind round his left hand. He was medium height, perhaps a little short of it. He kept looking behind him.

So it went on:

Dark hair—needs a shave and haircut—brown coat with patched elbows—the reports were too consistent for there to be any doubt.

By ten-thirty Roger was at his office at Scotland Yard. Peel was with him, and Detective Inspector Sloan, another big, boyish and powerful man, was also there. Two telephones kept going. Roger made more and more notes, and kept a third telephone free for outgoing calls.

"Get three men who saw this fellow up here as soon as you can," he said to Peel. "Have them go through the photographs in the Rogues' Gallery."

"Right."

"Have river police and our chaps and the city police ready, so that we can get moving as soon as we know where the motorboat stopped," Roger said a moment later.

"Right."

"If he went as far as the Pool and the docks, we're not going to have much luck," Roger mused, in a temporary lull. "See if they can still make tea downstairs, Jim, will you?"

"Okay," said Peel, and used the telephone again. "Coming up," he added.

Roger lit a cigarette.

"Half-past ten on a Sunday morning," yawned Sloan, his fair hair standing almost on end, and his blue eyes looking tired. "I'll bet Mary's still in bed."

"I'll bet Janet is, and the kids on either side of her," Roger said, and grinned. "She swears that she gets up early on the Sundays when I'm out of the house by eight, but I doubt it. It's just as well the girls don't know we've just been authorized to carry guns on this job. I— Here we go."

The telephone bell rang again.

"Hallo?" His pencil was poised, but he didn't use it. He stood up quickly, the others moved across to get their hats. "Right, thanks." He banged the receiver down. "Waterloo Bridge, south side," he said. "Come on, we'll walkie-talkie others to get there."

4

The Trap

Hundreds of police converged on the area about Waterloo Station. Dozens invaded the station and began questioning the station staff. It should be easy to find a young man with dark hair, in need of a haircut and shave, and with his left hand injured.

Other police rounded up known criminals in the area. Men who had gone off duty were interrogated. Now and again there was a false alarm.

Roger West, Sloan and Peel sat in a police car near the station, hearing the rumbling of the trains, watching the traffic as day trippers crowded the station entrances. The radio telephone was on practically all the time. The car was just a blue fog of smoke.

Then an authoritative voice came over the radio, with a sharp note that might have been excitement.

"I think we've got something—Pole Street, up round by the Elephant & Castle. A plain-clothes man was picking up a con-man, and saw a youth who might be our man go into Number 24. We could be wrong."

"How long ago?" Roger rapped back.

"An hour and twenty minutes."

"Surround the house at a distance, don't let anyone go too near. Anyone can go into a street, no one must come out of it without being stopped," Roger ordered. "Let them get round the nearest corner before stopping them."

"Right, sir."

"What are you waiting for, Jim?" Roger demanded, and grinned as Peel switched on the engine.

They drove fast toward Pole Street, which was ten minutes away. Three other police cars were already drawn up near the end of the street, and a dozen policemen stood about, but all were out of sight of the houses in Pole Street itself.

Two men hurried forward as Roger's car arrived, one a tall, thin, very dark man.

"Hallo, Raiment," Roger said. "How are you?"

"Fine, thanks." Raiment was a D.I. from the local Division, and the man who had sent the call. "If we've got the right chap, I can tell you something about him. He's been lodging at the house for several weeks. He keeps odd hours—two or three of our lads have noticed him getting home at four one morning. He was questioned once, and said he played in a dance band."

"Did he have any instrument with him?"

"A trumpet."

"Could be," Roger said. "Where's the policeman who questioned him?"

"At the station—he told me about this several

31

days ago. The youth's name is Prescott, Roy Prescott."

"Prescott?" Roger echoed, and for some reason thought of Neil Harrock and Ruth Linder; she was still fresh in his mind. He thrust thought of her aside. "Is anything known about the people he lodges with?"

"The man's something on the railways, at Waterloo. Youngish chap. The wife doesn't go out to work. There are two children, both toddlers."

"It would be worth getting in touch with your men who've seen Prescott get back late, and finding out what nights he was out," Roger said. "Then we could check if anything happened on those nights—armed holdups or bank robberies—you know what."

"I'll fix it," said Raiment. "How are you going to tackle Prescott now?"

"The simple way," Roger said. "I'll walk straight up."

"But—"

"We can have men approaching, keeping close to the houses on the same side of the street," Roger said. He looked along Pole Street, which was long, narrow and drab, with two-storied terraced houses on either side. A few children were playing in the street, one was cycling round and round aimlessly. "I'll look as little like a copper as I can." He took off his hat and flung it into the car.

"Don't forget he's armed," Sloan warned. "You ought to wait until we close in at the back, too."

"Five minutes," Roger said. "And haven't I got a gun, too?" It was heavy against his hip.

He lit another cigarette.

Five minutes later, keeping close to the houses

32

on the even-numbers side of the street, he walked toward Number 24. A line of plain-clothes men followed him; another line was coming along the street in the other direction. The back of the house was being closely watched by now.

The playing children stopped, to stare.

Roger walked briskly, still pulling at his cigarette.

A youth who had killed once might kill again.

The youth didn't know that he'd killed, though —couldn't be sure. But he had been prepared to kill. There were too many like him. They were young, ruthless, deadly—dangerous misfits in society. They were an anxiety to many of the public and a curse to the police. They weren't professional crooks and couldn't be tackled in the way that regulars could.

Few criminals he knew would shoot their way out of trouble.

Roger watched the windows of Number 24. There were cream-colored curtains at them; no curtain moved. Roger glanced up. No one appeared to be looking out of the upper window.

He waved to his men to stop where they were, and went forward on his own. Anyone watching from Number 24 could see only him, but the others would come rushing at any sign of need.

Roger stopped at the front door. It was freshly painted and varnished brown, with an iron knocker and an iron letter box. He knocked twice, not too heavily, trod out his cigarette and lit another.

No one answered.

He knocked more heavily. The sound echoed up and down the street. The children were all staring at him, so were several adults. There was a hush everywhere.

He knocked again.

Soon he heard shuffling footsteps, a child's voice, running footsteps. So it was normal enough. He drew back. The door opened, and a young woman wearing a red skirt, with a big shawl round her shoulders, opened the door. Her hair glittered like brass, and she had a pert, pretty face. Two small girls stood by her side. She clutched the hand of one, and held the shawl in front of her breast with the other hand.

"What is it?"

"Roy Prescott in?" Roger asked, very quietly.

"Who wants him?"

"A friend," Roger said.

"Okay, wait a minute," the woman said, and turned away. She pushed the door to. Roger put his foot forward, and it couldn't close. The woman looked at him sharply, but made no protest. She walked toward the flight of narrow stairs, with the child still clinging to her hand, and the other glancing from Roger to her.

"Roy!" she called in a strident voice.

An answer came at once, from a man who had obviously been listening.

"Who wants me?"

"Says he's a friend."

"Who—" Roy Prescott began again.

His voice was that of an educated man. He came from a room at the head of the stairs, and Roger first saw his feet and legs—and then saw that his right hand was bunched inside his trousers pocket; as it might be if he held a gun. His left hand was out of sight.

34

Roger moved forward, thrusting one child behind him.

"Keep still, Prescott, and don't—"

There was no time to finish. He saw the fist bunch inside the man's pocket. He flattened himself against the wall, and snatched out his own gun. He heard the roar of the shot as Prescott fired over the woman's head. The bullet smacked into the wall.

The woman screamed and grabbed the other child.

Roger had a clear view, and fired as Prescott took his gun out of his pocket for a second shot. The bullet caught the youth in the wrist. The gun dropped, clattering on oilcloth. The woman screamed again. The child behind Roger whimpered. A door alongside the stairs opened and a black-jowled man in his shirtsleeves came rushing out.

"What the hell—"

"Just keep still, Prescott," Roger said, and covered the youth with his gun.

Had Prescott another weapon?

Other police were rushing from the street.

"What the *hell?*" repeated the man hopelessly. He put an arm round his trembling wife. "Where's Doris, where—"

"Daddy!" screamed the child by Roger.

Prescott swung round and rushed toward the room he'd come from. Blood dripped from his right hand, and his left was heavily bandaged. Roger didn't hesitate, but fired at his legs; one shot was enough. As Prescott fell, Roger raced up the stairs, with other police streaming after him.

Prescott still had the strength and guts to squirm round, on the floor, and kick out.

"Don't made it harder for yourself," Roger said stonily, "or for anyone."

Prescott, lips turned back over strong white teeth, poured a stream of oaths at him.

Prescott was sent to hospital, with two police in attendance. He was in no danger, but it would be at least three weeks before he could get about again. He had refused to say a word, once he had stopped swearing.

The frightened woman, her husband and the children had quickly been shepherded into a downstairs room. Judging from their reaction, they hadn't known that Prescott was dangerous, although they'd probably known that he was a thief.

Roger, Sloan and the local man, Raiment, went up to Prescott's room.

In fact, there were two rooms; an archway had been knocked into the dividing wall. They were surprisingly well furnished. The bedroom had a double bed, a small wardrobe and a lot of photographs, mostly of girls. Powder and other oddments made it clear that Prescott didn't spend all his nights alone.

The other room was a kind of living room cum parlor. It was pleasantly furnished, with a portable radio in one corner and a 20″ table-model television in another. There was a square of Indian carpet and well-sprung armchairs. This was much more than the degree of comfort that Roger expected to find in a house in Pole Street.

Shelves of books were on either side of a gas

fireplace. Prescott had a wide range of reading; Maupassant was there in the original French. Everything suggested a young man of some culture.

"I wonder if he had time to plant the money from the bank anywhere else," Peel said.

"I shouldn't think so. Let's have a look round."

They opened cupboards and drawers, moved the books and shifted the furniture. For a few minutes, they found nothing.

It was Raiment who discovered a wad of notes, fifty or more, poked down by the side of one of the chairs. In a few seconds the others found more; until practically the whole amount stolen from Putney was found. Every possible hiding place had been used.

"Just about one of the quickest jobs we've ever done," Peel said, and grinned with satisfaction. "Cut and dried in a few hours. Here's another wad." He drew a wad of bank notes from behind some books. "I— Hal-*lo*."

In a recess behind a row of books he found two more automatic pistols.

"Let's keep at it," Roger said grimly.

They worked in silence, and with an increasing sense of strain. They found seven .32 automatic pistols, and at least a thousand rounds of ammunition; it was a small arsenal. A dozen knives were found, too, hidden in the most unlikely places.

There was a small box beneath floor boards in the parlor. Inside were rings, brooches, earrings and other small pieces of jewelry, all of good quality.

"He hasn't done so badly for himself," Raiment said, "but why seven guns?"

"That's worrying me, too," Roger said. "Let's try the bedroom."

They went through the archway.

Roger was telling himself that he didn't like the indications at all. Seven guns could make seven youths deadly, could make seven murderers. Prescott appeared to have worked on his own this morning, but here were the indications that he was one of a gang—at least, that he supplied others with weapons.

There was too much shooting; too many deadly youths.

"Nice lot of pretties," said Raiment, looking at some framed photographs on a table.

"Aren't they?" Roger agreed, and then concentrated on one photograph in an expensive gilt frame.

It was of Ruth Linder, looking at her loveliest.

5

Death in Hospital

Roger sat back in his car as Peel drove away from Pole Street. By then a crowd of several hundred had gathered, and there was a ragged, sardonic cheer as the car turned the corner.

Raiment and the local men had been left behind. Everything that had been found at the flat and was of interest to the police had been packed in a box and was already on its way to the Yard.

All the money taken from the bank at Putney had been recovered.

In the crate were the photographs, including that of Ruth Linder. Nothing else had been found to indicate that Prescott knew her. No diary, no records of any kind had been kept at the little house. Before being sent off in the ambulance, Prescott had been searched, and nothing had been found that incriminated him. The other couple, still being questioned, swore that they had not suspected that Prescott was a criminal; he had convinced them that he was in a West End dance band.

Sloan had gone with Prescott to the hospital;

and Sloan was in Roger's office when Roger reached the Yard. It was then nearly one o'clock.

"How is he?" Roger asked.

"They had to operate on the wrist, he won't be out of the anesthetic until late this afternoon," the detective inspector said. "Not well enough for us to question him, anyhow. But there's enough to work on with the crate."

That had already arrived, and Sloan had started to empty it. The photographs were lying face downward on one of the five desks in the office, which housed five chief inspectors. Sloan stood one photograph up, and looked at Roger deliberately, knowing what Roger thought about Ruth Linder.

"Going to talk to her?" Sloan asked.

"Not yet," Roger said, "but we can start working on her. Find out if Prescott's known at the Mile End Road shop or at the flat where she now lives. I don't feel like losing any time on this job." He lit a cigarette, and drew at it deeply, savagely. "I ought to be on top of the world, and I'm as dejected as I would be if I'd lost a fortune." He ran his fingers through his hair. "We'll try again to make Prescott talk, but I don't think he will. He's tough." Roger's lips curled. "Like a lot of them."

"If only we still used the cat—" Sloan began.

"Look, let's keep out of that argument," Roger said, and went across to the crate. "We want to identify all the women, and identify all the jewels. If we can find out what jobs Prescott did before this one, it would help. If we can find out where he sells his stuff, it would help more." He glanced at Ruth's photograph, and spoke to it. "I told you I'd get you if you carried on the old man's business, didn't I?"

"Roger," Sloan said, "remember all those kids she goes around with. She doesn't have a steady, but is always out with a different kind. Kid's the word. How old would you say Prescott is?"

"Twenty-two or three."

"Younger than Ruth Linder?"

"Yes. Same age as Neil Harrock," Roger said. "He was hanged, too. Prescott will be hanged. But Ruth's settling down, isn't she? She spends a lot of time with Hann-Gorlay."

"She still sees the others."

"I don't like this at all," Roger grumbled. "It isn't an isolated case of robbery with violence. Prescott did the bank job brilliantly, and knew exactly how to do it. He had nitroglycerine which went off before he'd got behind the safe for cover and that's what led us to him—but he'd been taught. A killer-thief with a private arsenal and access to nitroglycerine. The most important thing is to find his buddies-in-crime, and the only way I can see is through the girl friends. Don't lose any time on that."

"Not a minute." Sloan picked up the telephone.

"Isn't anyone around here hungry yet?" Peel asked.

"We'll go and have some food soon," Roger said offhandedly, and lit a cigarette.

He looked at Ruth Linder's photograph again. The past months had done something to her. Her beauty had gloss, her hair was beautifully set, the whole effect was one of class. She had been with a millionaire at the Majestic—a millionaire who was also a politician and a believer in harsh punishment for violent criminals. She also knew Prescott—if that photograph meant anything, it meant that. She hated the police, and had inherited a business of buying and selling stolen jewels.

Roger thought about her a lot that day.

Other thoughts also tugged at his mind.

The greatest worry was the seven .32 automatics. There were known to be a lot of service revolvers about, but automatic pistols weren't so freely available on any market.

Allenby had been killed with a .32.

So had at least one other policeman, on a case he had investigated himself.

He rang Records.

"We've had several attacks on policemen this year, Records; can you tell me what guns were used each time?"

"Half a mo'." Roger held on; it proved to be for two or three minutes. "You there, Handsome? Point 32's, all five of 'em."

"Thanks," said Roger heavily.

He stared at a report in front of him, without reading it, then drew a slip of paper toward him and scribbled: *have all gunsmiths warned to take special precautions against robbery and burglary—check any losses they've had—where considered necessary by local police, arrange special watch.*

He pushed the paper aside.

Ruth Linder came into his mind again.

He simply could not find any evidence that she knew Prescott, apart from the photograph.

Otherwise, the routine investigations went well. Three of Prescott's girl friends were found; each swore that she knew nothing about Prescott being a thief; each wore jewelry that looked expensive.

Each was watched. No male friends of the injured prisoner were found that night. Some of the jewelry found at Pole Street was identified as part of hauls made in the central London area.

Roger and Sloan checked the case history of the robberies concerned and the tallies of the stolen jewels.

"If Prescott took it all," Roger said when they had finished, "he's disposed of three parts of it. Bill, I think we'll raid the Linders' shop in the Mile End Road. We can find some excuse. The Divisional men can do it, then no one will think we're behind the raid."

"I'll fix it," Sloan said.

"Who's managing it for Ruth Linder now?"

"The same fellow who took over when she moved up in the world," Sloan said. "Sol Klein. Sol reminds me of Old Benny, you know. He's got the same manner, the same smoothness. Unctuous. It won't do any harm to give him a shock."

Roger nodded.

"Think you'll be able to talk to Prescott tonight?" asked Sloan.

Roger shrugged.

By five o'clock he knew that the doctors would allow him to talk to the prisoner later in the evening. That gave him a few hours to spare. He handed everything over to a night-duty inspector, and was driving toward his Chelsea home by half-past five.

He turned into Bell Street, a wide road with small, detached suburban houses on either side. It was pleasant and friendly; practically everyone in the street knew him; he nodded and waved to several neighbors as he drove along. He had hardly stopped outside his house when the front door opened and his two sons came tearing toward him, Martin—sometimes called Scoopy—the elder boy, was yards ahead. He was nearly ten, could have passed for thirteen, and had a grin as wide as a Cheshire cat's.

"Hallo, Pop; jolly glad you're home!"

"I'll pop you, you young—"

"Hallo, *Father*," greeted Richard. He was a head shorter than Martin, nothing like so massive, and had a smaller face which could become impudent at a moment's notice. He had sky-blue eyes, and ears which stuck out almost at right angles. "How's the crime business today?" he inquired.

Roger found himself laughing.

Janet, his wife, came hurrying down the stairs. She was dark-haired, a beauty to him and attractive to any man, and delighted that he was home earlier than she had expected.

He felt that warm satisfaction which came from being home. The murder of Allenby, the shooting at Pole Street, the viciousness of Prescott, all seemed to fade. That was a different world, a different life.

By half-past eight the boys were on their way to bed.

"We could leave them for an hour," Roger said, "and you could come along with me to the hospital, where I have to talk to a bad man."

"I'd love to," said Janet. "But I don't like leaving them here alone."

"Hang it, Scoop's ten—"

"They're very young," Janet objected. "And when you read the newspapers, there seems to be nothing but cosh raiders and crimes of violence."

"You read the wrong newspapers! See if any of the neighbors can come in for an hour."

"You're not going to be long, are you?"

"I shouldn't think so."

"I'll stay here," Janet decided.

Roger left the house a little after ten o'clock. Janet was worried, as most people were, by the unmistakable crime wave. It was easy to say, even to think, that it was exaggerated by the popular Press; it remained a fact that there was a hell of a lot too much violence. Roger knew the answer; so did every other man at the Yard—a police force of twice its present strength. That was like asking for the moon, but everything else was simply a palliative.

He drove up to the front entrance of the hospital, parked the car, hurried up the steps. He didn't expect to get anything more out of Prescott, but there was always a hope. If he could get a line on Ruth Linder, it might help.

He knew the hospital well, and tapped on the Night Sister's door.

"Come in," she called.

He looked in.

"Everything all right?"

"Oh, yes; you can go along and see him," the Sister said. "One of your men's there; the other's having a snack."

"Nurse trouble?" Roger asked, and grinned.

The Night Sister laughed.

Roger walked along slowly. He couldn't get that picture of Ruth Linder out of his mind; it went with him everywhere. He tried to reason why. He often thought of her a great deal, and finding the photograph had given point to his uneasiness. She was clever, she hated the police, and Roger had no reason to think that she had any moral scruples.

He reached the door of the ward, which was in a wing of the hospital, on the first floor, and where all injured prisoners were sent from the Yard or the nearby Divisions. He didn't tap, just went in.

He felt as if he had run into a brick wall.

Prescott lay on his back in bed, with a wound in his forehead. The man from the Yard was on the floor in front of his chair—and his head lay in a pool of blood.

The window was smashed.

The horror clutched and held Roger tightly for several seconds. No one was about. Everything was silent. If it were not for the bullet hole in his forehead, Prescott would have looked as if he were asleep.

Roger went forward slowly, knelt beside the policeman, felt for the pulse, and satisfied himself that the man was dead. He couldn't have been dead more than ten minutes.

Footsteps sounded along the passage.

The other Yard man came hurrying. He turned into the room, and stopped. His mouth opened, but he didn't utter a word.

Roger said in a flat voice, "Stay here. I'll call the Yard."

He called the Yard, then Janet to tell her that he wouldn't be home until late, then the AZ Division, which covered the Mile End Road. The Linder shop had already been visited. Sol Klein had given them all possible assistance, they had found nothing that was stolen, nothing to suggest that the old

46

business of buying and selling stolen goods was being carried on.

"Thanks," said Roger.

He rang off, and went back to the ward. The hospital staff knew what had happened by then. Doctors and nurses were in the ward, and tension was in the air.

Roger sent for searchlights, had them trained on the window, brought ladders, checked how the murderer had got up to the window. That had been fairly easy. There was a big drainpipe, and many windows with strong stone ledges. Any nimble-footed youth could have climbed up. No one had heard the shooting.

There were no fingerprints.

The only clue was a few strands of dark gray woolen cloth which had caught in the joint of the drainpipe. They had been torn from a coat or trousers, and were obviously new. Roger sent them to the Yard, but there was too little for analysis. They could make out the texture of the wool, guess the kind of suit it had come from, but probably never be sure—unless they found the suit within the next day or two, while the little tear in it was fresh.

By twelve o'clock the routine work was finished.

By half-past Roger was driving along Bell Street again. There was no light on at his house. A car was parked a little way beyond it, with the parking lights on. He saw a tall, shadowy figure moving from this car toward the gate of his house. He felt a sudden tension—the kind which had gripped him when he had seen the two dead men. He hadn't fully recovered from that shock.

He put his hand to his pocket, snatched it away,

then swung the car into the drive, switching on his headlights. They shone on a familiar face—Brammer's, of the *Courier*.

Roger felt the keen sharpness of relief, and that told him how keyed up he was.

Janet had left the garage doors open. Roger drove straight in, then switched off the headlights. Brammer sauntered up the drive, and stood and waited as Roger turned the key in the garage door.

"Now what?" Roger asked mildly.

"Stand me a whisky, and I'll tell you something you don't know about Prescott," Brammer said.

6

Ruth Again

Roger opened the street door, and stood aside for
Brammer to enter. As he followed the newspaperman, Janet called out from upstairs:

"Is that you, Roger?"

"Won't be long, darling."

"Don't stay down there," pleaded Janet.

"I've someone with me, but I won't be long."

"All right." Janet didn't sound pleased.

Roger switched on the hall light, and then that
of the front room. Here the furniture was exactly
the same as when he and Janet had married, except for one or two new oddments. It had a slightly
worn, comfortable look. His armchair had its back
to the window, with the radio beside it. Janet had
put the whisky and soda out for him, on a table by
the chair. There was only one glass.

"Sit down," Roger said, and proffered cigarettes,
then fetched another glass and poured out.

"Thanks." Brammer's hooked nose and thick lips
gave the reporter the old, familiar sardonic look.
He was good at his job; in fact he was brilliant.
There were those who thought that he had a chip

on his shoulder—just as Ruth Linder had. His heavily lidded eyes were dark and very bright. "Just a splash of soda," he added, and curved his thick lips as he sat down and stretched out long legs. His big brown shoes hadn't seen polish for days.

Roger handed him his glass, and raised his own.

"Cheers."

"May the hangman never run short of rope," Brammer said.

"What's this you know about Prescott?"

"He's a boy friend of Ruth Linder."

Roger sipped his drink again.

"Sure?"

"I'm quite sure."

"How do you know?"

"I've seen him with her," Brammer said. "He's a natty dancer, and she likes to dance. She's always dancing with nice-looking boys, well-educated kids from good-class families, too. She didn't do much dancing before her uncle Benny died, though. I suppose you knew something about all this?"

Roger nodded.

"Sorry if I've wasted your time," Brammer half sneered.

"If you're sure about Ruth Linder and Prescott, you haven't wasted any time. Can you prove you're right?"

"You just have to take my word. Has Prescott talked?"

Roger said, "No." He looked at the reporter closely. Brammer was good; and might be expected to know what had happened at the hospital. Fleet Street knew by now. But was there any

50

reason why Brammer should pretend that he didn't? "He won't either," Roger added.

"Say, what's this?" Brammer asked sharply.

"He was shot and killed, as well as one of my men. The killer climbed the wall of the hospital."

Brammer hadn't known; his eyes showed both the surprise and the shock. He sat very still, with the glass in one hand and the cigarette in the other. Then he said quietly but clearly:

"Handsome, how many policemen have been shot this year?"

That was easy to answer.

"Five, before Allenby and my man tonight."

"And how many coshed? Or attacked with some weapon or other?"

"Probably another five or more."

"There've been nine coshed," said Brammer. "Making sixteen attacked in all. They see something suspicious, go to investigate, and are shot or coshed. Handsome, you know that the *Courier's* been going all out in the crime-wave business and is campaigning for harsher punishment, don't you?"

"I'd have a job not to!"

"It's going to start running another angle," Brammer said. "It's an angle I've put up to the boss. I don't think you're going to like it."

Roger didn't speak.

"It's going to draw attention to the similarity of the attacks on the police," Brammer went on. "It's going to show that at least half of them, and probably more, have been made by youths. It's going to show you that every bullet taken out of a policeman this year had come from the same-sized

51

gun—a .32 automatic pistol. Weren't they all .32's at Pole Street?"

Roger said slowly, "You get your facts right. I'd noticed the bit about the policemen, too. What else is the *Courier* going to say?"

"It's going to suggest that there is a deliberate campaign against the police—a terror campaign. It's going to show that a policeman's life isn't so safe these days. It's going to campaign for better salaries, a big recruiting drive, and—guns for the police as regular issue."

Roger finished his drink.

"And is it all your idea?"

"No, mine's the bit about a terror campaign against the police."

"What's your evidence?"

"What I've told you, plus the fact that Ruth Linder hates the police and has these boy friends —the tough type who probably carry guns. There isn't any doubt that she knew Prescott." Brammer emptied his glass.

"Another?"

"Thanks."

Roger refilled the glass, and gave himself another whisky, but added plenty of soda.

"Why come and tell me?"

"You always play ball with us," Brammer declared, "and although you probably won't admit it, you collect most of the really dangerous jobs that are going. You handled this morning's job brilliantly—it's one of the slickest the Yard's ever done, and the *Courier* will say so!" Brammer gave his sardonic smile. "It's also going to suggest that, from now on, your life isn't safe. After the hospital killing, that will look a lot more plausible, won't it? *I'm* going to say that you should carry a gun all the time, and so should everyone connected with the Prescott case. I'm also going to say that nothing else is likely to warn these young brutes off."

"I see," said Roger.

"Care to comment?"

"I would not!"

"Off the record, then."

"You wouldn't let me down about that, would you?"

"No."

"I don't care what they do on the Continent or in the United States. I don't think it would be a good thing if we were armed. We've never armed our police except on special jobs. If our police carried guns, more of our criminals would arm themselves. There'd be more, not less, violence; more risks—and not smaller ones either. Larger."

"That's just the official attitude," Brammer said, as if disappointed.

"It's personal opinion," Roger assured him, "and it doesn't mean that I don't think we should ever carry arms. There are times when I'm much happier with a gun. As this morning! But if we have an armed police force, before we know where we are we'll have an army of armed bandits."

"We've got one."

"For every crook in this country who carries a gun, hundreds don't," Roger said. "And you know it. Anything else?" he asked abruptly.

"No, I don't think so," Brammer said. "The blatt's going to scream at the top of its voice about this, and the other papers will take it up."

"You have to find something to write about,"

Roger growled. "You heard my wife complaining, didn't you?"

Next morning the *Courier* came out with the first broadside of the campaign for "improving the efficiency of the police." It was one of the papers which Roger had delivered to Bell Street, and when Janet came into the bedroom with the post and papers, she was reading it. Roger did not like her expression.

"If you'd been in that ward last night—" she began.

"But I wasn't, my sweet!"

"I suppose you'll just go on until one of them does shoot you," Janet said. "The boys were reading this when I went downstairs. And this about the campaign against the police by these young terrorists, too. Do you think there's anything in it?"

Roger said, "I suppose there could be. I wouldn't put it higher."

"Does that mean that you know there is?"

"It just means that I think there could be," Roger repeated, and slid his arm round her shoulders. "I don't think there's any reason at all to say there is, yet. Even if there were a campaign, it wouldn't last long. A few more raids like the one we made on Prescott's place, and they won't have any weapons left."

Janet's body didn't yield against him.

Within an hour of reaching the Yard, Roger sensed the "atmosphere." It had been there the previous morning, when the news of P. C. Allenby's death had been spread. It was created every time a policeman was murdered, or whenever the Yard was under exceptional pressure from the Press. But this time it seemed more tense.

It affected Sloan and Peel.

There were those who said that Brammer and the *Courier* were talking out of their hats; but others agreed, either by comment or by silence, that they were right. Several were all for being armed; more, for flogging and severe corporal punishment as well as imprisonment.

At half-past ten, Roger's telephone bell rang.

"West speaking."

"Come and see me, will you?" The gruff voice was that of the Assistant Commissioner at the Yard, Sir Guy Chatworth. "And don't take all day about it."

So the atmosphere affected Chatworth, too.

The A.C. was a big, burly-made man with a ruddy face, veiny skin, a shiny bald patch surrounded by grizzled hair and a soft blue collar that was a size too large for him. His office was a modern wonder of black glass and chromium. He sat at a huge glass-topped desk, looking rather like a sulky bulldog.

"Good morning, sir." Roger was bright.

"Sit down. You can smoke if you want to. What about this terror campaign?"

"It's much too early to give an opinion," Roger temporized.

"I wonder. Trouble with you, the trouble with all of us, is not seeing the wood for the trees. A lot of people have talked about a terror campaign in the past few weeks—but not a single policeman has. I've pooh-poohed it where I could, without being happy about it. That hospital shooting—" Chatworth broke off.

Roger lit his cigarette.

"That was to keep Prescott quiet—it wasn't part of any campaign."

"But you think there is one, don't you?" demanded Chatworth.

"No," Roger answered. "I simply think there could be."

"What do the others say?"

"There's a feeling that there is a campaign," Roger admitted. "I get a queer impression, sir— that most of our men suspected it subconsciously and that this newspaper howl has brought it to the surface. I still think it could be wrong."

He told Chatworth about Brammer's visit; and the story of Ruth Linder.

"Do you think she's capable of organizing this?"

"I think she's worth a lot of watching," Roger told him. "I also think we could jump to conclusions far too quickly."

"So long as you don't jump too late, all right. You know there isn't a chance in hell that the Home Office will let you fellows carry guns as a general practice, don't you?"

"Yes."

"But you and anyone working with you on this case can carry a gun all the time," Chatworth went on. "Whether there's a terror campaign or not, there was a killer at that hospital last night, and we want him. Your job, Roger."

"Thank you, sir," Roger said. "But as for carrying a gun all the time, I don't think—"

Chatworth leaned back, opened his center

drawer, took out an automatic and two clips of ammunition.

"Take this," he said abruptly. "Carry it all the time. That's an order. You're in charge and you might be a target any moment."

"Yes, sir," Roger said stonily.

Brammer had told him that he got the dangerous jobs; Janet said the same thing. Well, he did. He could even persuade himself that he liked them, but as he walked back to his office, he knew that he didn't. P. C. Allenby and the Yard man with Prescott had been alive and kicking until a moment or two of seeing a man with a gun. Yet he didn't want a gun all the time. At heart, he was sure that it would lead to trouble. What the police needed was new recruits by the thousand.

But he had his orders, and Janet would probably be glad.

He could leave Janet and the boys, get into his car, drive off—and be taken back to Bell Street soon afterward, ready for a coffin. Death was always near, and this job brought the fact close home.

Nothing else had come in from the hospital; they had no clue apart from the pieces of wool, which weren't much help. Sloan and Peel were checking Prescott's girl friends one at a time, with help from the photographs found at Prescott's flat. Apart from Ruth Linder, he had seen more of a girl named Weston, Pauline Weston, than anyone else. A man recently moved into the plain-clothes branch because he had shown exceptional ability as a shadow was put on Ruth; his one job was to follow her, and to report and describe everyone whom she saw, day by day.

It wasn't quick and it wasn't satisfying.

The *Courier* ran the terrorist campaign story by itself for three days. On the fourth two other London dailies took it up. The atmosphere at the Yard became more turgid than ever. There was a curious sense of waiting for anther attack on a policeman.

On the evening of the fifth day, P. C. Babbington, of the KJ Division, was patrolling that part of St. John's wood near Regent's Park. It was dusk. Several people were in sight, all of them moving briskly. One youth walked toward Babbington, perhaps more quickly than the others.

He was dressed in a tweed jacket and baggy trousers, and was hatless.

As he came almost level with the policeman he drew a gun from his pocket and fired three times into Babbington's face. Babbington fell, dying instantly. Someone shouted. The killer broke into a run, until he reached a motorcycle resting against the curb.

He was astride this, and near the first corner, before any of the horrified passers-by reached the policeman.

7

Visit

Roger West opened the *Courier*. He stood quite still, looking at the front page. The boys were on the stairs. They stood and watched, very quiet.

Janet was still upstairs.

TERROR STRIKES AGAIN
ANOTHER POLICE VICTIM

Terror struck again in familiar, friendly London last night. A 53-year-old policeman, well liked by his neighbors, loved by his wife and children, was patrolling a street near the Zoo.

A killer shot him down.

There was no reason for it. The policeman was by himself. The killer was not being questioned. Here is further evidence that there is a deliberate reign of terror aimed at London's heroic police force.

In common fairness the men who protect us must be armed.

"Is it another one, Dad?" asked Martin.

Richard looked straight at his father's face,

without echoing the question. Martin's gray eyes were rounded, candid, untroubled.

"Yes, Scoop."

"It's awful, isn't it?"

"It's not very good."

"Mum hates it," Richard declared.

"I expect she does, old chap."

"There's one thing," Martin said; "you don't wear a uniform, Dad, do you? There's a chap at school, Bob Arnold, his dad's a sergeant at Chelsea, perhaps you know him. Bob Arnold says that *his* mum hates it, too."

"She would," said Roger.

The boys weren't old enough to talk like this. Nine and ten—and talking of terror, fear, the danger of wearing a uniform, walking hand in hand with the horrors of sudden death. It was hideous. In the past they had often been excited and thrilled because he was a detective. This case had sobered them—and the sobering had not come abruptly. It must have been growing in them, through Janet perhaps as well as through Bob Arnold's "mum," for some time.

"Why don't these men *like* policemen?" asked Richard, looking impossibly angelic. "Policemen are nice men, aren't they? Why, they see the young kids across the road every day at our school; they're ever so nice. It's silly to shoot them."

"Ridiculous," Martin agreed solemnly.

"Boys," said Roger, "nip into the kitchen, put the kettle on for breakfast and cut the bread for toast, will you? You'd better light the gas, Scoop."

"Oo, I can do it just as well as Martin!" Richard forgot police and gunmen as he rushed to get into the kitchen first.

Roger looked up at Janet, who was on the landing. He had seen her standing there almost from the moment the boys had started talking.

Janet hadn't spoken about the Yard when Roger had got home, late, on the previous night.

"So there's another one," she said, when he reached her. "Let me see." She scanned the headlines. "It is true, you know, Roger. It's a campaign."

"If it is, it'll be beaten."

"But—" began Janet, and then her chin went up, her voice hardened, and she turned briskly toward the stairs. "I must go and get breakfast. I know there's nothing you can do about it; I only wish you'd never been idiotic enough to join the police force."

She ran down the stairs.

There was another item of news, too. Residents in Wimbledon and Putney were calling a meeting to form a Citizens' League—its purpose to demand harsher punishment for violent criminals, and an armed police force.

That would have interested Roger by itself, but there was an item which reminded him vividly of Ruth Linder. Her handsome and wealthy friend, Sir Neville Hann-Gorlay, had been asked to speak at this meeting.

Roger tapped at the door of Chatworth's offices, and went in. Chatworth was on the telephone. He waved to a chair, and sat in silence with the receiver at his ear. He listened so long that Roger guessed that he was talking to a superior—probably someone at the Home Office. Even the superior could not keep Chatworth quiet for long when he disagreed.

"Balderdash," he growled.

He listened again, fidgeting in his seat.

"Addlepated imbecile," he spat.

He kept quiet for fully thirty seconds.

"Congenital lunacy," he roared. "Can't stay now, I'm busy. Call you later!" He banged the receiver down, glared at Roger, then stretched out for a small cigar and lit it. *That* was the Home Office."

"Was it?" Roger was mild.

"In the considered opinion of one of the permanent officials, too much attention is being paid to this terror campaign talk."

Roger grinned, in spite of himself.

"We're going to have a lot more talk before long. The *Courier* has now lined up four other morning and two·evening papers as well as a dozen or so in the provinces, all wanting revolvers to be issued to every man on the beat. It'll get stronger until some other sensation chases it out of the headlines."

"Still against guns as normal issue?"

"I'll willingly take a gun when I'm likely to tackle a gunman, but I prefer not to otherwise," Roger said. "I've been testing opinion on the subject here, sir. It's about evenly divided. I wouldn't much care to say what it will be if there are many more jobs like this St. John's Wood one. Being shot at while stopping a crook has always been an occupational risk. Being shot while patrolling is a different matter. I've had Peel trying to get the feeling of the uniformed staff, too."

"What is it?"

"They're all being harried by their wives," Roger gave the ghost of a grin. "Ninety-nine in a hundred say they want the cat back, and harsher treatment generally."

"What you really mean is that everyone's getting edgy."

"Yes."

"Any ideas?" Chatworth asked abruptly.

Roger said, "It could be a simple vendetta, but I find that hard to believe. I keep after Ruth Linder. We've got a kind of line to her again. A Charles Mortimer, one of the youths Ruth has entertained at her Mayfair flat, is going about with a girl who knew Prescott. The girl has some jewelry which was probably stolen. I think I'll have another look at the stuff, and if it is stolen, hold the girl for receiving. That should make her talk."

"Anything's worth trying," Chatworth agreed. "If it isn't a simple vendetta, what the hell is it?"

Roger shrugged. "I couldn't work up an idea if you offered me a thousand pounds! Have you seen that bit about a protest meeting at Putney and Wimbledon?"

"Citizens' League, or some such nonsense?"

"If the public get really worked up about this," Roger said, "it's going to give us a lot of new problems."

He left Chatworth soon afterward, and went to see Pauline Weston, Prescott's favorite girl friend after Ruth Linder. Pauline Weston also knew the youth Mortimer. It was almost a forlorn hope; but everything had to be tried, some seeming trifle might open the case wide.

Pauline Weston was tall, ash-blond, slim, almost flat-chested, but with much grace of movement. She wasn't exactly a beauty, but had a certain attractiveness—and her gray eyes had a pleasing candor. She wasn't more than twenty-two or -three,

63

didn't overdo make-up, and dressed simply, mostly in tailored clothes.

She lived in a two-roomed flat in Bayswater. By profession a research chemist, she did no regular work and appeared to have private means.

She opened the door to Roger, who handed her his card. She smiled quite impersonally.

"Won't you come in?"

"Thanks."

He went past her into a charming flat of pale blues and gold, chintzes, all very comfortable. It was eleven o'clock in the morning.

"How can I help you, Chief Inspector?"

"Do you know a man named Charles Mortimer?" Roger's manner was friendly enough.

"Yes."

"Do you know him well?"

"He's only an acquaintance," Pauline Weston said. "I've known him for several months."

"How did you meet him?"

"I suppose you'll expect to hear this," she said. "I met him at a party which Roy Prescott gave."

"How well do you know him?" Roger looked straight at the brooch at her throat. It was of diamonds, worth several hundred pounds, and in a beautiful platinum setting. She couldn't fail to notice that he was studying it. "Does he ever give you presents?"

"No," Pauline Weston smiled faintly. She spoke well, seemed to be of good breeding, appeared to be frank and in no way hostile—perhaps slightly amused. "I *bought* this brooch from Charles, Chief Inspector."

"Really? How much for?"

"One hundred and five pounds."

"May I see it?" asked Roger.

She took it off and gave it to him, outwardly quite unconcerned. Her poise might be assumed, but seemed to Roger to be genuine enough.

"Thanks." He examined the brooch by the window, where the light made the diamonds scintillate; vivid colors flashed from the tiny facets. It was worth at least four hundred pounds. Roger couldn't be sure that it was stolen; but P. C. Allenby had been shot, and Babbington was dead; this wasn't the time for half measures. "Did it occur to you that this might be stolen property, Miss Weston?"

"It did not." She was still quite cool, but he thought that there was a sharper gleam of interest in her eyes. "Are you sure?"

"It looks like part of a haul stolen several weeks ago. Other pieces from it were found at Prescott's rooms," Roger said. "How long have you had this?"

"About a month."

"I'll give you a receipt for it," Roger promised, "and take it away with me to check. When did you last see Charles Mortimer?"

"Two nights ago."

"Do you know where he is now?"

"I haven't the faintest idea."

Roger didn't say much more. The girl raised no protest about him taking the brooch, went with him to the front door and closed it on him.

He went noisily down the stairs, but didn't go out of the house. He waited for a moment, then tiptoed up the stairs again, knelt down and pushed the letter box open.

"Charles, don't be a fool," the girl was saying; "I tell you he'll come round at once. He's got the

brooch....Yes, he's by himself at the moment....
Well, I've warned you."

She rang off.

Roger went downstairs on tiptoe. The girl had
tried to fool him, and had a cooler nerve than
most. She must have been at the telephone as soon
as the door had closed. He could picture her as
clearly as if she were by his side. Tall, composed,
too thin, with nothing much in the way of a figure
but with an almost exciting grace of movement.
She had a mind, too, and had hidden her thoughts
well.

She was inches taller than Ruth Linder, fair as
Ruth was dark, with the looks and beauty of an
English rose; compared with her, Ruth was an ex-
otic orchid.

Roger grinned at the thought.

If Pauline Weston played this kind of game, she
would soon have some of the poise shaken out of
her. He did know where he was with Ruth, but this
girl—

A taxi pulled up, and a man appeared at the
door, opening it before the taxi stopped. It was
Brammer. He jumped down, thrust a hand into his
pocket for some money, then caught sight of Roger.
He went still for a moment, then paid off the cabby
very deliberately, turned, and gave his thick-lipped
grin.

"Who've you been third-degreeing this time?"

"You tell me," said Roger.

"So you won't talk, huh?" Brammer's grin became more sardonic as he went into the house.

To see the English rose? If he'd got on to Pauline
Weston by a different route from Roger, it
strengthened the need to watch the girl closely.

The speed with which Brammer was on the spot in his job was quite remarkable.

Roger reached his car, and spoke to the detective officer who stood by it.

"Recognize the chap who just went in there?"

"Wasn't it Brammer of the *Courier*, sir?"

"Right first go! Make a note of how long he stays and whether Miss Weston leaves with him. Follow the girl, not Brammer. If she takes a cab or uses a car, phone the Yard at once, giving the registration number and vehicle description. All clear?"

"I've got it, sir."

"Good man." Roger slid into his car and picked up the radio telephone. The Yard answered promptly.

"Detective Inspector Sloan, please.... Hallo, Bill, listen. Pauline Weston has just telephoned Charles Mortimer, to warn him I've been questioning her. Mortimer's one of the lads who's been running around with Ruth Linder. He might cut and run for it. Watch his flat. As soon as he leaves, we want to move in to search. If he runs, we'll have him followed."

"What's the idea?" Sloan asked.

"If Mortimer goes on the run and Ruth Linder's in any way responsible, he might go and see her. I'm going to her flat, and I'll watch it from the car. Have the Division warned and ask them to watch the Mile End Road shop. If Ruth should turn up, radio me."

"Right," promised Sloan. "But aren't you forgetting something?"

"What's that?"

"Ruth Linder's being watched by Jackson, the new boy from the uniformed branch."

"If she leaves before I get there, he'll be gone too," Roger pointed out.

He rang off and drove straight to the block of luxury flats in Wilmington Place near Park Lane. It was a large, white block with small balconies outside most of the black iron-framed windows.

Almost the first man he saw was Jackson, the "new boy"; so Ruth was at home. Jackson was big and ruddy-cheeked, eager-eyed, alert-looking in a smart navy blue suit and new gray trilby.

Roger drove past, catching the detective's eye, and turned the corner. Jackson came up at once.

"If Ruth Linder comes out, don't follow her but follow me," Roger ordered. "And if I go into the building, give me a quarter of an hour, then come and see what's doing."

"Right, sir!" Jackson's tone underlined his enthusiasm; this was his chance and he meant to take it.

Roger maneuvered the car so that he could see the entrance to the flats, and waited. Five minutes later, Ruth appeared at the entrance as a taxi turned into the far end of Wilmington Place. It stopped, Ruth got in, and the cab moved off again at once.

Roger followed.

It wasn't long before he knew that they were heading for the East End.

He had time to think, and seeing Ruth so quickly after the other girl made further comparison inevitable. Rose and orchid? Pauline Weston was the taller by several inches, but the great contrast was in the different bearing. Pauline was calm, casual, almost aloof. Men would look at her first because of her grace of movement, then be charmed by her face, but wouldn't think much about her figure.

Men would be caught and excited by Ruth's figure, only to be disturbed by the smoldering fire in her beauty.

The one connecting link was their acquaintance with Charles Mortimer, friend of Prescott, who had sold Pauline a piece of jewelry far below its proper value.

8

About Face

Traffic was thick, and the cab in front of Roger was skillfully driven, squeezing between towering buses and huge lorries, nipping past traffic lights. Roger kept pace with it until they were on the other side of Piccadilly Circus; then a bus which cut across him hid the taxi from sight.

He didn't pick it up again.

He pulled into the side of the road and flicked on the radio. He didn't see Jackson behind him, but thought nothing of that.

"...yes, sir," a man at the Yard told him. "Charles Mortimer left his flat five minutes after you telephoned, and he's being followed. The last report we had was that he'd reached Fleet Street."

"Keep broadcasting his movements," Roger said.

He didn't switch off, but put the receiver on the seat by him, and listened as he moved into the traffic again. He couldn't hear plainly. In every traffic block or chance to slow down, he picked the instrument up.

"...Mortimer passing St. Paul's in green M.G. sports car."

"...Mortimer at the Bank of England."

"...Mortimer passing Aldgate Station."

There was no longer any reasonable doubt that he was heading for the Mile End Road. Had Ruth Linder come along here, too? There were several taxis, but none with the number of hers. Jackson wasn't in sight, either. Had he seen a chance of glory, and followed her after Roger had been baulked?

Roger saw plain-clothes men from the Division patrolling the road opposite the shop. He slowed down near it. There was no taxi, but a green M.G. car stood outside.

Men across the road recognized Roger, and nodded; one man came hurrying.

"Mortimer's been in there for ten minutes, sir. Ruth Linder's only just arrived."

"Good."

"Going in, sir?"

"Yes."

"Be careful."

"Yes," said Roger, "I'll be careful."

The warning was a trifle, but it meant a lot. Three months ago the Divisional man wouldn't have thought of saying that; the possibility of danger wouldn't have occurred to him. He was a hefty fellow, and wouldn't lack physical courage.

Roger looked round.

He still didn't see young Jackson. That began to worry him. Jackson might be anxious to hide from Ruth Linder, but there was no need to keep in the background while she was in the shop, and he should have shown himself.

"Want anything, sir?" the Divisional man asked.

"One of my men ought to be behind me," Roger

71

said. "Big, ruddy-faced young chap—keep an ey[e]
open for him."

"I will."

Roger went briskly toward the shop.

The windows were very different from what the[y]
had been in the days of Old Benny. Instead of [a]
mass of junk, seldom taken out, tidied or dusted[,]
they were dressed brightly enough to compet[e]
with any jeweler's shop. Some of the stock looke[d]
good. Half of one window was taken up with china[,]
the other half with silver plate and bric-a-brac[.]
Everything had a polished, well-cared-for look.

Roger opened the door.

The interior, which had been gloomy in the ol[d]
days, was now almost too bright. Two fluorescen[t]
strip lights on at the far end accounted for that[.]
The bell at the door clanged, and Roger was hardl[y]
inside before a young man stepped out of a room
at the back. He was plump, tall, well dressed, i[n]
dark clothes, handsome in his swarthy way. H[e]
came hurrying rubbing his pale hands together[,]
his flabby face wreathed in smiles. This was So[l]
Klein.

"Why, Mr. West, what a pleasure! How are you[,]
Mr. West?"

"I'm fine. Is Ruth here?"

"Why, yes, Mr. West, but what would you wan[t]
with Ruth? She—"

"Listen, Sol," Roger said; "this isn't a game. G[o]
and tell her and Mortimer that I want to see them[.]
Tell them that the shop is watched back and front[,]
and that it won't pay either of them to get up t[o]
funny business."

"Really, Mr. West, I don't understand you," So[l]
said earnestly. He looked anxious and puzzled, bu[t]

kept smiling; he was always excessively anxious to please and to reassure. "She's with the boy, yes; but I don't see why you should expect trouble."

"Go and tell them, will you?"

"Well, all right, all right," Sol said. "Of course I will."

He hurried along the shop and up the narrow staircase.

As voices came from the room on the right at the head of the stairs Roger recalled that night when he had come here to see Old Benny. Sol Klein went up the stairs two at a time. His legs were long, and he had an athlete's ease of movement in spite of being overweight.

"Ruth, just a minute—"

"You get to hell out of here!" That was Mortimer. "This is between me and Ruth."

"Don't be silly," Sol rebuked him. "Ruth, Mr. West—*Chief Inspector* West—is downstairs. He says he wants to see you, and that the place is watched back and front."

Mortimer said, "What the devil *is* this?"

"Nothing you need worry about, Charles," said Ruth Linder.

Her voice startled Roger. It was deeper, fuller— a fine, carrying voice, much more attractive than he had know it before.

"I'm not so sure—"

"You can be sure."

"You mustn't keep Mr. West waiting too long," Sol said agitatedly.

"Bring him up, Sol."

"All right, my dear, all right."

Sol turned, and saw Roger at the foot of the stairs. He smiled brightly, and beckoned.

73

Roger went up slowly.

"Did you or didn't you know that brooch was stolen?" Charles Mortimer demanded in a tense voice.

"Of course I didn't," said Ruth. "In fact, I don't think it was. The police do make mistakes, Charles. Don't they, Mr. West?"

She must have heard Roger enter, for she was facing the youth and the window, and didn't see him. As she spoke, she turned and smiled.

It was like being smiled on by Circe up-to-date. At close quarters, she was magnificent. She wore more make-up—or a more expert make-up. Her hair was beautifully set. Her dress was green, simple perfection drawing attention to the provocative line of her breasts. Her hat probably cost a fortune, she looked like a million pounds. There wasn't a hint of hostility in her manner or voice as she went on:

"Or don't you ever admit to error?"

"Oh, we've been known to slip up," Roger conceded.

"And you accept the possibility! You see, Charles, the police aren't necessarily ogres. Are you sure that the brooch you took from Pauline Weston was stolen, Mr. West?"

"No. I haven't had it checked yet."

"When you have, I'm sure you'll find that it was honestly come by. Charles—I mean Mr. Mortimer —bought it from me, and gave it to Miss Weston. He was most upset when it was suggested that it was stolen." Ruth moved to a small table in a corner, and picked up a box of cigarettes. "Won't you smoke, Mr. West?"

Roger took a cigarette. "Thanks."

Mortimer waved the box away. He was a tall,

dark-haired youth, not bad-looking, but rather intense—as if he had been keyed up for a long time. Judging from his clothes, he wasn't short of money.

"You've no right to go round saying that people have stolen goods in their possession!"

"That's the last thing I'd do," Roger said. "If Miss Weston had been a little more patient, I'd have told her as soon as I knew the truth about the brooch. She didn't object to me taking it away, you know."

"Why the hell did you need to pester her?"

"She knew the man Prescott—he was murdered, and he had stolen jewelry in his possession," Roger said formally. "Is it all right with you if we do our job?"

"Don't you go about frightening girls who—" Mortimer broke off.

"Did you know Prescott?" Roger asked.

"Supposing I did."

"*Did* you?"

"We'd met."

"Where?"

"What the devil has that got to do with you?"

"Charles, you'd be wise to answer Mr. West's questions," Ruth Linder interrupted. Her voice was honey sweet. Her eyes were glowing, as if this amused her but she didn't want to let the boy realize it. She was baiting Roger, and putting everything she had into it; as she did into everything. "The police never ask questions unless they've a good reason. Do you, Mr. West?"

"We like to think we've a reason."

"Where did you meet Roy Prescott?" Ruth asked the youngster.

Mortimer growled, "Don't be silly, you know."

"And I don't mind who else does, Charles." She gave a little laugh. "They met at my flat, Mr. West. I throw a party every now and again, and a friend brought Roy Prescott along to see me. Charles happened to be there at the same time. All quite innocent, you see."

"I see," said Roger. "Let me get this all straight, Mr. Mortimer. Miss Weston telephoned to tell you that I had inquired about the brooch which you sold to her, and you came here to find out why Miss Linder had sold you a brooch which might be stolen. Is that right?"

"Yes," Mortimer growled.

"If it wasn't stolen, I'll have the brooch returned to Miss Weston within an hour or two," Roger said. "Now I want a word with Miss Linder alone, please."

Mortimer glowered. Mortimer was very young, and seemed to be furiously angry. "All right," he growled, and went to the door. "Sorry if I made a fool of myself, Ruth."

"Oh, it wasn't you who made a fool of yourself," Ruth said sweetly.

Roger grinned.

Mortimer reached the door and was going out, when Roger called:

"Oh, one small thing. How much did you pay for that brooch, Mr. Mortimer?"

"That's my business."

"Tell him, Charles," urged Ruth.

"Eighty pounds," Mortimer said abruptly. "So I didn't exactly make an extortionate profit, did I?"

He stalked out of the room, and they heard him

go down the stairs. A moment later, Sol Klein spoke to him soothingly.

Roger stubbed out his cigarette.

Ruth Linder sat on the arm of an easy chair, her beautiful legs crossed, her right arm bent and on the back of the chair, thrusting her breasts forward; seductively?

Roger had never felt so convinced that he was being fooled.

He took the brooch out of his pocket, and the diamonds scintillated. He carried it to the girl, and held it in front of her eyes. She didn't shift her position.

"It's lovely, isn't it?" she said lightly.

"It's worth two hundred pounds, even in the trade."

"Yes, I suppose it is."

"Why did you sell it to Mortimer for eighty pounds, if you bought it legitimately?"

"I rather like the boy."

"Listen, Ruth," Roger said, and took out his own cigarettes. "I don't want to be difficult. I don't dislike you personally. But I warned you what would happen if you started dealing in stolen goods. Where did you get this brooch from?"

"Sol bought it," Ruth said, and laughter lurked in her eyes. "A wholesale and manufacturing jeweler was going out of business, and Sol was able to take a lot of his stock at very low prices. So I passed the benefit on to my friends. Sol will have the receipt; you made a mistake about it being stolen. A deliberate mistake, I imagine." Her eyes mocked and her body called to him as she moved from the chair to the window. "I run a completely honest business, Chief Inspector. You're only wasting the valuable time of your men having them watch me. I should have thought you'd much more important work to do."

"Ruth," said Roger.

"Yes, Chief Inspector?"

"You can be too smart—much too smart. But you can't be too careful."

He went toward the door.

She seemed to watch him with eyes which danced with wicked laughter. She followed him downstairs and into the shop, and held his arm lightly, pressing against him. Roger opened the door as a taxi pulled up.

Brammer got out.

Until that moment, Ruth had filled the whole horizon. Ruth, deliberately trying to stir him to interest, to admiration—to desire? He was acutely conscious of her—until Brammer arrived, with his remarkable timing.

Roger lit another cigarette, and watched him; wondering.

"An expensive day in taxis," he observed.

"The *Courier* spares no expense, Handsome!" Brammer gave his crooked smile, but that faded as he turned to Ruth. "Ruth," he said very softly. "Keep your claws off Pauline Weston. Understand? Keep your nasty little boy friends away from her." He glanced at Roger, and went on, "Pauline and I are getting along fine. Ruth doesn't like to think I should have fun. You're witness that I've warned her off."

He turned and stalked away.

78

9

Warnings

Roger let Brammer's taxi go before he went outside. The hatred between Brammer and Ruth was really something if that brief interview meant what it seemed to. Roger was almost persuaded that Ruth would try to hurt Brammer through the girl.

Pauline Weston. . . .

She was too young for Brammer, surely—although she had the maturity of her breeding, and a gravity which in some ways matched Brammer's.

Roger went out.

Jackson wasn't outside the shop; by now he most certainly should have been. The Divisional man hadn't seen anyone answering his description. Roger persuaded himself that the D.O. had probably lost the trail and done the sensible thing —gone back to Wilmington Place. His disappointment would be quite desolating; he couldn't be keener.

Charles Mortimer would undoubtedly be trailed back to his flat—which should have been searched by now.

"Need us here any longer?" Roger was asked by Divisional men.

"No, I don't think so, thanks."

He went straight back to the Yard, then sent a man to see if Jackson were outside the flats in Wilmington Place. He was on edge about Jackson, but by no means sure that there was any good reason for it. His nerves weren't as steady as they should be.

He went to see Gillick, the Yard's expert on precious stones. Within five minutes Gillick was able to tell him that they'd no record on the stolen list of a brooch like the one he'd taken from Pauline Weston.

"Just a little mistake of yours, Handsome—we all make 'em!"

"That's right," said Roger dryly.

He slipped the brooch back into his pocket, deciding to return it himself. He still had the uneasy feeling that he had been fooled.

The *volte-face* of Ruth Linder worried him most.

He went back to his office, and made a kind of table of events in which she had been concerned. It started with the hanging of her father and the suicide of her mother; reason enough to cause bitterness. It was the kind of thing which might easily give rise to a neurosis—might drive hatred and bitterness deep into a mind, and warp it.

Until Old Benny's death, her manner had suggested that bitterness was warping her mind.

Her behavior at the time of her uncle's death had certainly borne that out.

Then she had begun to change. It had first shown when she had left the shop in Sol's hands and moved to the luxury apartment. There had been a succession of young boy friends, all of the stamp of Prescott and Mortimer, but no one had seemed to stake any claim on her.

Soon afterward, she had started to move in a completely different society, Hann-Gorlay's world. She carried it off well. She would be a hit in any social gathering. She had poise, intelligence, wit and beauty—but all the bitterness seemed to have gone. There was nothing to connect her with the attacks on the police and the so-called terror campaign, except the fact that she had these many youthful boy friends and had known Prescott.

Now she was selling jewelry very cheap to the lads.

She was making plenty of wealthy friends, too. *Was* it just that she had changed, and had become a social climber?

Why had she gone to the shop to meet Mortimer? It would have been easier for her to wait at Wilmington Place.

The thing to remember, Roger told himself, was that whatever she did she would do with that deep vitality; she would put everything she had, wit, looks, body, into success.

The telephone bell rang.

"West speaking."

"Sergeant Hall here, sir. I'm speaking from a kiosk near Wilmington Place. Detective Officer Jackson isn't here."

"Oh. Sure?"

"Quite sure, sir."

"Hang around for an hour, then report again," said Roger.

He put the receiver down, found himself lighting

a cigarette mechanically, and then grabbed the receiver again.

"Give me Sloan....Hallo, Bill, listen. Jackson followed me but didn't turn up in the Mile End Road, and he's missing. Have all squad and patrol cars and stations notified, will you, for a general lookout for him?"

'Yes. Funny business, isn't it?"

"Funny's one word," Roger growled. But at least Ruth was out of his mind for a while.

When Hall reported again, there was still no news of Jackson, although Ruth had returned to her flat. No word came in from the patrols or Divisions. It added to the tension; it would add a lot more when the news got round the Yard. It would be easy to overdo the anxiety though. There might have been an accident, Jackson might be in hospital.

Roger couldn't loaf about, waiting for news.

Pauline Weston was on his list, and Brammer's remarkable timing, almost as if he had some sixth sense, wanted investigating. How well did Brammer know Pauline Weston?

Roger went to see the girl again.

She was on her own, calm, perfectly poised, apparently ready to be quite frank. She said she had known Prescott and Charles Mortimer for several months, but not really well. She had not bought anything from either of them until this brooch. She didn't know any of Mortimer's other acquaintances.

"How long have you known Mr. Brammer?" Roger asked.

"For several weeks," she said, and her eyes

gleamed. "He told me you would probably want to know. We have a lot in common."

"Such as?"

"Wanting to stop this banditry."

"You keep out of it," Roger warned her grimly.

He left the flat thoughtfully. The girl had made an impression on him; she was right for Brammer, with a maturity greater than her years. There was no intensity about her; in fact she was almost too casual. He wasn't quite as sure about her flat chest, now; she had quite a nice little figure, and fine, clean lines.

He called the Yard on the radio telephone. There was no news of Jackson.

Jackson still hadn't turned up that evening.

Nothing had been found at Charles Mortimer's flat; the gambit had failed completely. Ruth was probably laughing with mocking delight at his wasted time.

When he left the Yard, at half-past seven, Roger found himself on edge, half fearful of news of another attack on a policeman. None came; but he knew that there were others as much on edge.

He wasn't in the right mood for going home. Janet would soon discern just how he was feeling, and that wouldn't help either of them. He drove to AJ, the nearest Divisional Headquarters, and talked to the Superintendent.

"Any of your fellows feeling a strain, Josh?"

"Well, that's putting it a bit high," he was told. "But they'll be glad when all this has blown over." The Superintendent was large, fat, comfortable and comforting. "As I say to 'em, who could possibly have any reason for putting our backs up? It just doesn't make sense."

It made sense that he had to reason with his men.

Roger drove to another Division and found the same atmosphere; edginess and anger rather than tension. There was another thing, too—determination to get the thing over as quickly as possible.

He made his last call at the nearest Division to Bell Street. Sergeant Arnold, whose son was at school with Martin and Richard, was stationed here.

The Superintendent, Christie, was a lean, brisk confident man.

"No doubt it's getting under the skin of some of the chaps," he said. "I've arranged for them to patrol in twos in certain parts of the Division. Wise precaution, I think."

Roger didn't challenge it; or say that it was obviously a concession to fears that Superintendent Christie wouldn't voice.

When Roger got home, Janet was tired, didn't seem inclined to talk much and didn't mention the subject which he was sure was on top of her mind.

He lay awake for some time, hoping that the telephone would bring news of Jackson. He wasn't disturbed. In the morning Janet seemed brighter, the boys were boisterous, and Roger promised to take them to school in the car. He was about to leave when the telephone bell rang.

"Hallo?"

"Christie here," the man at the other end of the line said. "Can you look in on your way to the Yard this morning?"

"Yes," said Roger, "in twenty minutes or so."

He wondered why; it was an unusual request and almost certainly arose out of the call last night.

The boys squeezed on to the front seat, and the nearer they got to the school, the more frequently they waved to envious friends. Neither of them seemed to notice that Roger was much more preoccupied than usual.

It was only five minutes' drive to the police station from the school.

Christie jumped up from his desk as Roger entered his office.

"Don't know whether you've had any others of these," he said jerkily. "Sergeant Arnold got this this morning." He handed Roger a letter—a single sheet of white paper.

"Letter" was a courtesy word for it. There was a single line of typing, no address, no signature— just the one sentence:

LIFE ISN'T VERY SAFE THESE DAYS, IS IT?

"*Have* you heard of others?" Christie demanded.

"No," said Roger, very slowly. "Not yet. Where's Arnold?"

"On his way up—I told him to come as soon as you were announced." Christie glanced at the door, and there came a heavy tap at it. "Come in."

Arnold was a plumpish, middle-aged sergeant, the solid old-fashioned type.

" 'Morning, sir." He touched his helmet.

"Hallo, Sergeant," Roger said. "Has your youngster gone to have his usual scrap with mine this morning?"

Arnold grinned, pleased.

"Young rips, they are!"

"Yes. What time did this come?" Roger held up the note.

"Morning post, sir," said Arnold, and the grin faded. "I don't mind telling you, I was glad I got it first, and the missus didn't see it. There was another letter, too, so she didn't smell a rat."

"Had anything like it before?"

"No, sir."

"Any special reason why you should have had it? You haven't been attacked or threatened in any way, have you?"

"Everything's been normal, sir," Arnold said—"that is, as far as anything *is* normal, these days. Want more flogging, that's my belief; we're too soft with the swine."

"A lot of people agree with you," Roger temporized. "I'll take this—thanks." He waited until the sergeant had gone, then asked Christie, "No prints, I suppose?"

"One set—same prints as on the other envelope Arnold had this morning. He had the sense to bring both along, for testing. So we can say that the only prints on that were the postman's." Christie sat back in his chair, and looked very bleak. "I'm beginning to think there *is* something in this idea of a terror campaign."

Roger shrugged. "So's Arnold," he said.

He drove too fast on the way to the Yard, left his car at the foot of the steps, and hurried up into the Criminal Investigation Department Building. Everything was normal—fool, why shouldn't everything be normal?

86

He strode into his own office.

Three other chief inspectors were there, including Eddie Day, the Yard's forgery expert. Eddie was an unhealthy-looking fifty-odd, with a growing paunch, prominent teeth and weak-looking eyes. He had a fishlike appearance which would have been familiar on a fishmonger's slab or a butcher's block.

"Hallo, *Handsome!*" He had some difficulty with his aspirates, and when he achieved them it was always with faint emphasis. "What d'you make of this turn-up?"

The other C.I.'s were looking across at Roger.

"What one? Have they found Jackson?"

"No—don't say you *haven't* 'eard," breathed Eddie, excitement driving the hard-won aspirate dying. "Why, most've the Divisions 'ave 'ad threatening letters. There's dozens of reports."

"All saying the same thing," broke in another C.I. "*Life isn't very safe these days, is it?*"

Roger stood very still.

The telephone on his desk rang.

"Bet that's Chatworth; been after you for the last twenty minutes," Eddie brayed. "Shall I answer—"

Roger moved to his desk.

"No, thanks." He lifted the receiver. "West speaking."

"There's a gentleman on the line for you, sir," said the operator, "but he won't give his name. Will you speak to him?"

"Yes."

"One moment, please.... You're through, sir."

"Chief Inspector West speaking," Roger said.

A man laughed; the sound wasn't very loud, but

87

it was very clear and had a nasty note. Then the man said smoothly:

"Life isn't very safe these days, is it, West?"

The line went dead.

10

Campaign

Roger put down the receiver slowly. The others stared at him. He lit a cigarette, as Eddie Day burst out:

"What's up, 'Andsome? What was that?"

"They use the telephone as well as the post," Roger said, and forced his voice to sound relaxed. "Did you say the Old Man's been after me?"

"Yelling 'is 'ead off, I told"—Eddie drew a deep breath—"I told him I'd let you know as soon as you came in. You're to go straight to his hoffice. Oh, ter 'ell with ruddy aitches!"

Roger found himself smiling, but his lips felt tight.

"You're all right, Eddie." He sat at his desk and called Sloan. "Bill, how many of these letters have been reported?"

"Seventeen," Sloan said promptly. "We've heard from thirteen divisions where they've had one each—always a sergeant, by the way—and from four departments here—Records, Fingerprints, Information and Civil branch. All uniformed, too, no plain-clothes men."

89

"Have you got the letters?"

"Chatworth sent for them."

"Right, thanks," said Roger. "Jackson?"

"Not a word."

Roger said, "Was he married?"

"No. Roger, who hates us like this?"

Roger didn't essay an answer, but rang off.

Eddie Day fidgeted because Roger was keeping the Assistant Commissioner waiting....

Chatworth was grave, not in one of his ranting moods. It was a bad situation. There could now be no argument about what was happening. And:

"If we could find a reason, Roger, I'd be happier. I can't see any sense in it."

"No one can yet," Roger said.

He fingered the envelopes—seventeen in all, each with the letter inside. A report with them said briefly:

1. No fingerprints on letters, those on envelopes probably postmen's.
2. Paper all the same make, a thin bond, sold in practically every Woolworth's and cheap store in the country.
3. Each has a City, E.C.3 postmark.

"Not much in these, either," Roger growled. "Going to let the newspapers have this, sir?"

"What do you think?"

"It would be a mistake not to. If they discovered we were hiding—"

The telephone bell rang.

Chatworth lifted it, grunted, grunted again and said, "Wait a minute," and handed the receiver across to Roger. "It's Sloan."

Sloan wouldn't interrupt him in this office, unless this mattered.

"Hallo, Bill?"

"There's a squeak about Jackson," Sloan said. "Either that or a trick, Roger. We've had a letter by post, saying we'll find him at a house in Hammersmith."

"Let's get there," Roger breathed. "Don't lose a minute."

They found Jackson.

He had been shot through the head with a .32 automatic.

The *Courier* had the biggest and blackest headlines, on the front page; and the front page was given over to the story completely.

TERROR CAMPAIGN GROWS
OPEN THREATS TO POLICE
ANOTHER YARD MAN SLAUGHTERED

The story itself was hardly worth reading. There was the usual "We must arm the police" demand, and a list of prominent public men and women who supported the move—and the Citizens' League—and a smaller list of those who opposed it.

Every newspaper had the story of the letters to the policemen. Every Division in the London area and a number in the Home Counties had had one, but no Division had received more than one.

Roger glanced at the telephone when it rang—and felt a momentary qualm. Eddie Day and the other C.I. in the office paused to look up.

"West speaking."

"Spare me a few minutes, Handsome, will you?" It was Brammer. "I'm here at the Yard."

"Yes," said Roger. He didn't want to see the *Courier* man in the office, with Eddie Day listening in. "I'll come down."

He went down and took Brammer to a waiting room.

The *Courier*'s inquiry man hadn't shaved, and his stubble was more gray than his hair. His eyes were red-rimmed and looked glassy, his hooked nose had never seemed more prominent. As he dropped into an armchair, it became hard to see him as Pauline Weston's mate.

"Glad you give your guests comfort! Off the record, are you any nearer finding out who's behind all this?"

"No."

"Listen," Brammer said. "I may be wrong, I may be crazy, but I still think it's Ruth Linder. I know she's leading a gay life these days, but I think she's behind it. She still hates. No one else *could* have been sure that Jackson was a Yard man, could they?"

"Let's say she could have known."

"There's a man who might give you what you want," Brammer said. "That's Sol Klein. If you scared him enough, he'd talk. Work on him, Roger."

"I was hoping you'd have something more than a guess," Roger said.

"Listen," said Brammer earnestly. He lit a cigarette, looking at Roger. "She's got all these boy friends. They sell jewelry at cut prices for her. That doesn't make sense in itself, but it's true. They're the same type as Harrock and Prescott—they could become killers, even if they're not. The important thing is that they'll do almost anything that Ruth asks them to. I think she's fencing on a much bigger scale than her uncle ever did, and that she's laughing her head off because you can't prove it. She's just making a fool of you. She's even dangling Hann-Gorlay on a piece of string, because of this Citizens' League business. She—"

"Six months ago—" began Roger.

"I told you that I know she's happier," Brammer reminded him heavily. "I know she's changed; but why not? She's having the time of her life. You're fooled, all the police are getting worked up. She must know that. Why, in several Divisions they don't patrol in ones any longer, they go about in pairs! Everything Ruth ever wanted she's getting. Why shouldn't she feel on top of the world?"

"Give me anything I can use as evidence, and I'll act."

"I spend half my time looking for it," Brammer confessed. "Ruth sleeps late in the mornings and stays up half the night. So I look half dead." He drew deeply on his cigarette. "How do you feel about it?"

"Oh, I enjoy it," Roger said dryly.

"Sooner or later she's going to turn the heat on you personally, because you put her uncle inside the last time. But she'll get a kick out of seeing you dancing about like a flea on an elephant first. *Any* ideas at all?" Brammer asked abruptly.

"I told you," said Roger. "No."

Brammer shrugged, and kept silent.

"What worried you so much about Ruth and Pauline Weston?" Roger asked mildly.

"I just don't trust Ruth as far as I can see her,"

Brammer growled. "She hates my guts—she'd gloat over seeing my girl friend in trouble." He grinned, savagely. "I had quite a lot of bother with Pauline, after telling Ruth to lay off."

"Why?"

"Pauline thinks it would be a good idea if she kept friendly with Charles Mortimer and got to know some of the other boy friends Ruth amuses herself with."

"You keep Pauline out of trouble," Roger advised, still mildly.

"You'll have to try." Brammer showed a kind of sardonic amusement. "She's determined to help. It isn't all her fault, either. She knows a man who really feels badly about the crime wave—a lawyer named Matthewson. Have you heard of him?"

"Vaguely."

"You'll be hearing more," Brammer said. "Matthewson seems a mild-mannered little middle-aged johnny, but he's dynamite. Hann-Gorlay's a forceful personality with plenty of money. Together, they'll form a kind of vigilante organization, still calling it the Citizens' League, and—"

Roger said sharply, "That's only talk."

"Don't you believe it," Brammer seemed to leer. "Vigilantes will relieve the police of a lot of work, won't they?"

"It's crazy. They'll make these young brutes worse—make 'em more reckless."

"Not on your life."

Roger said, "I tell you it's madness."

"Well, try to stop it," Brammer said.

Roger didn't speak.

"You know you can't," Brammer went on, "unless you can put an end to the campaign. Which brings me to Ruth again. She's even thicker than she used to be with Hann-Gorlay—and getting a bigger laugh. Take it from me, she's behind this. But I wouldn't like the job of telling Hann-Gorlay so."

Brammer left an obvious question behind him—why was he so anxious to damn Ruth Linder? Why did he hate her—why should she hate him?

The question went further. Was Brammer drawing a red herring across his own trail? If so, he was doing it clumsily, and he wasn't the type to be clumsy.

Roger put two men on to finding out whether Brammer had any particular association with Ruth or with her uncle. The only association Roger knew about was that Brammer had been a cub reporter at the trial of her father.

He put Detective Sergeant Peel on to probing further into that almost forgotten case.

"Dig everything out, Jim. Find if her father had any other relatives—how old he was when he died —were there any other children. I still can't believe that this is a vendetta, but we'd better find out what we can."

"I'll drop everything else," Peel promised. "Are you going to keep a man watching Ruth all the time?"

"Yes—and he must be armed," Roger said. "How do you feel about things?"

"I'm just angry," Peel told him quietly. "From the time I wake up till the time I go to bed, I'm bloody angry. That's how a lot of the fellows are feeling. But this swine's clever. He's got us by the short hairs, in a way."

"What way?"

"Well, look," said Peel. "First of all these letters go round. Every Division gets at least one. So everyone's keyed up. Then Jackson gets killed. Then—nothing. Everyone just waits. And a lot of the chaps don't find it all honey when they get home, either. The newspapers make their wives pretty touchy. *I've* never known anything like it. It would be better if we could keep the papers quiet for a bit."

"They'll calm down," Roger said.

Peel shrugged.

The suspense of waiting to see what happened after the delivery of the letters reached its peak twenty-four hours after he had first seen one. Except for Jackson's murder, nothing had happened. Everyone was feeling the strain, Sloan no less than anyone else.

"The screech is getting worse, and it'll get louder yet," Sloan said to Roger. "There's hardly a newspaper which hasn't joined in. Why the hell should anyone try to force the police to take up arms? That's what it looks like, but it just doesn't make sense."

"Whoever's behind it is probably pretty sure the Home Office would never issue the order. And Parliament wouldn't approve, anyhow." Roger was brisk. "Someone means to scare the lights out of us, and the idiotic thing is that they're succeeding. Do you know what the Chief's done today?"

Sloan said, "No."

"All security inside the Yard is tightened up. All passes have to be countersigned. No stranger is allowed in the Yard, whatever his introduction, without a severe screening. Chatworth's trying to make sure we don't get a smack in the eye from the inside. I—"

His telephone rang.

He listened, said, "Yes, all right," and rang off. "That was Brammer of the *Courier*," he told Sloan. "He says he's got something at his office he'd like me to see. I'm going straight along."

"Going alone?"

"Don't you start," said Roger.

Yet on the way he found himself looking round cautiously; watching cars which drew close to him, watching youths on racing cycles and men on motorcycles. The tension was in him, as it was in everyone.

The entrance to the editorial offices of the *Courier* were in a side street which led off Fleet Street. There was room to park his car. He pulled up, switched off and started to open the door.

Two men appeared, one on either side of the car. One slammed the door on Roger, the other got in beside him.

"Don't say a word, don't make any trouble," the man ordered, and the other got in the back. "We're armed. Drive on, go down to the Embankment, then over Blackfriars Bridge. Not too fast. No tricks, mind."

Roger felt something hard press into his ribs.

11

Long Chance

Roger sat motionless.

If he struggled, they would probably shoot him. The pressure against his ribs grew harder and more painful. It might not be a gun. He couldn't be sure. A new pain stabbed at his neck—not severe but unmistakable—the cut of a knife.

He winced.

"Just drive on, West."

The voice in his ear was the man's behind him. The touch of the knife came again, a sharp, searing cut; a moment later there was a curious warmth—blood flowing.

Roger switched on the ignition.

The moments of shocked horror had passed, and its paralysis with it. He could think; if they had intended to kill, surely they would have killed without taking this chance?

Why think that? Why not remember Jackson, with bullet holes in his head, lying in an upstairs room in a little empty house, his body stiff with *rigor mortis*? Something like this must have happened to Jackson.

A crack of his elbow against one man's rib, a jolt of his head against the other, and he would have a chance. He only needed time to fling the door open and get out.

He started the engine.

"West," said the man by his side, "see that little car behind—the red Morris?"

It was close behind Roger's Rover, in the mirror.

"If you try any tricks," the man said, "it will run you down. Don't make any mistake at all; just drive to the end of the street and then left on to the Embankment, and then across Blackfriars Bridge. You needn't hurry and you needn't dawdle."

He had a cultured speaking voice; and he was young.

Roger put the car in gear, and eased off the clutch. The car moved forward slowly. The man behind him had moved back a few inches, and was out of reach of Roger's head if he jolted it back. So the odds were heavier than they had been. He'd missed his chance. At least, he had missed one chance, but there was another—that the pair wouldn't kill.

The longer he was with them, the better his chance of finding out more about them.

He nosed the car into a stream of traffic behind a huge lorry loaded with massive rolls of newsprint. They crawled along the street, past the tall buildings of two of Britain's biggest newspapers. He saw three people whom he knew, newspapermen who would have taken wild risks to rescue him, just to get this story.

They passed.

"So Brammer is in this racket," he said.

"Shut up, and just drive."

"Are you the men who killed Prescott?"

"I told you to shut up." That was the man by his side, pressing the gun.

Roger said swiftly, furiously, "Who the hell do you think I am? I can smack us into the back of that lorry or into traffic on the Embankment or even into the Thames, and you two wouldn't have a chance in hell to stop it."

Neither of them spoke, for fully a minute.

They passed the newspaper buildings and reached the Embankment. Traffic lights were against them.

"Well, why don't you?" asked the man in the back.

"I can't stop you guessing," Roger growled.

They were puzzled and less sure of themselves.

Roger turned left, and then swung right on to Blackfriars Bridge. It was crowded with traffic, all moving fast. Soon they were driving along the wide road beyond the bridge, past small warehouses and large ones, small shops and cafés and side streets. The little red car followed. There was a lot of heavy, slow-moving traffic here.

Roger had a dozen chances to draw up alongside policemen or to crash and give himself a chance. He took none of them.

If he stopped, they would almost certainly shoot —and he wouldn't be the only victim. He might live, and others might die. That was one but not the chief reason for doing what they told him. There was a long chance that they didn't intend to kill—yet; that they had some other reason for this holdup.

The traffic thinned, and speeded up.

"See that yellow van?" said the man by his side abruptly.

"Yes."

"Turn right just beyond it."

Roger slowed down. Traffic was coming the other way, and he had to stop. He put his arm out of the window to signal as the red car also stopped. He felt the pressure at his ribs and the sharp cut against his neck again. Both men were keyed up—and in such a mood they would be trigger-happy.

He turned into the side street, which was deserted except for one or two vans parked without their drivers.

"Slow down."

Roger eased off the accelerator.

Then he sensed the change in their mood, in the tempo of events. Fear burned through him like a white-hot flame. He had no time to move or act. He felt a hand brush against his head, his hat was tipped over his eyes, a blow was smashed on the back of his head. The man at his side leaned over and grabbed the wheel.

A second blow crashed on Roger, and he was swallowed up in blackness.

Bill Sloan looked at the clock in the big office which he shared with other Detective Inspectors. He scowled. His big, fresh-colored face and startlingly blue eyes were unfamiliar because he was worried. He lit his pipe and looked at the clock again.

The door opened and Peel came in.

"Any news?" Peel asked.

"Not a squeak."

101

"Two hours and a half," Peel said, and left it at that.

"I wouldn't mind the two hours plus," Sloan said, "but he hasn't been to the *Courier*, and Brammer hasn't been in the office all the morning. I've had a call out for Roger for an hour, and not a squeak. I'll have to tell Chatworth, soon."

"This is how it happened to Jackson," Peel said, "Why the hell does Roger always have to stick his neck out?"

"It looked normal enough," Sloan argued. "He was sure it was Brammer. He's seen a lot of Brammer over this business. Have you learned anything more about him?"

"Not much. He's a Birmingham man, graduated on a Birmingham weekly paper, came down here and free-lanced on the Street twenty years ago. He did a good write-up job on the murder case where Ruth Linder's father was convicted, became a private eye and hasn't looked back. The *Courier* pays him a fortune. Have you tried his home?"

"Yes," Sloan said. "I've tried everywhere and anything I can short of raising the alarm. I don't want to do that yet, for a lot of reasons. Janet West isn't the least of them. I—"

The door was flung open, and Chatworth strode in; "stormed" suited his entry better. He was massive, burly and furiously angry. His face was red and his eyes glittered.

"Where's Chief Inspector West?" At his worst, Chatworth was always formal. "I've been trying to get him for the past hour." His small, bright eyes bored into Sloan's. "No one seems to know where he is."

Sloan, already on his feet, drew a deep breath.

"No one does know," he said, and fear touched them all.

During the night, Roger's car was found in a car park in the City; there were only Roger's fingerprints on it, and no clues.

It was ten o'clock, and Bell Street was quiet.

Janet stood between the boys' beds. Both boys were fast asleep. She could just make out their faces and their heads against the pillows, for light came in at the window from the street lamps. Martin was making queer little puffing noises, Richard slept with hardly a sound.

Janet gritted her teeth, fought back tears and went out and downstairs.

Bill Sloan was in the living room, standing and holding a whisky and soda, like a big, self-conscious schoolboy with a scowl on his ruddy face. Even when Janet came in, he couldn't get rid of the scowl and pretend that there was no real need to worry.

"Only thing I can say," he muttered, "is that it's happened before. The trouble is that Roger's always hitting the headlines. The devils make a beeline for him if they want to cause a sensation."

"As if I didn't know," Janet said. She was very pale, anguished, bitter. "Night after night I wonder if he'll come back. I sit here, waiting. I hear cars coming along the street, and feel like screaming when they pass. I can't help it, Bill, I hate it. Just now it—it's ten times worse than ever, but it's been going on for years."

Sloan pulled at his pipe.

"He's always pulled through."

Janet closed her eyes, then stiffened. A car turned into Bell Street, and they could hear the engine as it dew nearer. Both stared toward the window, both waited tensely for any softening in the sound of the engine, any sign that it was slowing down.

It went past.

Janet moved across to Roger's chair, and took a cigarette from a box. Sloan hurried to light it. Janet blew smoke out.

"I'll be all right, Bill. I'm sorry I feel so bad about it. It's this beastly campaign. It's always pretty nerve-racking—well, it's liable to be at any time, and a thing like this makes it worse. Mary must be feeling almost as bad as I am. Most of the wives, too. But it's all right, you know; we realize that you've got to find out who's doing it, you can't all resign!" Her voice became a little shrill. "Don't worry about me, Bill."

"Just in case it makes you feel easier," Sloan said gruffly, "we've put a couple of men in the street and a couple at the back. Not that I think there's going to be any trouble here," he added, and turned almost beetroot red. "It's just that we thought you might feel happier."

Janet gave a funny little laugh.

"Yes, Bill. Thank you," she said. "Oughtn't you to go home?"

"When we've found Roger," Sloan said, "I'll go home."

Sloan looked at the clock on the wall of the office. His eyes were red-rimmed and glassy—they hardly looked like the eyes of a real man. His big face was lined with strain. There were lines at the

104

corners of his lips, too, and whenever he spoke his voice was harsh; grating.

It was twenty-four hours after he had seen Janet. Since then he had seen nearly everyone connected with the campaign, including Ruth Linder and Brammer's girl friend, Pauline Weston. He had learned nothing new.

The telephone bell rang.

Two other D.I.'s, both on night duty, looked across at Sloan as he took the receiver. His body seemed to tighten up, as if there was an added strain on his taut nerves; and on his face there was a new tension—of hope.

"Sloan speaking."

"Any news?" It was Chatworth.

The fact that hope was deferred again showed vividly in Sloan's manner. He relaxed, but it wasn't the relaxation of relief.

"No, sir."

"Anything about the newspaperman, Brammer?"

"No, sir."

"Sloan, listen to me," Chatworth said. "These are orders, understand? Go home, go to bed; don't show up again for at least ten hours."

"Yes, sir," Sloan said, as if he'd no feeling in his voice.

Chatworth rasped, "I said they were orders!"

"Yes, sir," Sloan said.

" 'Night," grunted Chatworth.

He rang off. Sloan pushed his fingers through his stiff hair, and stood up slowly. He took his hat off a peg, turned and raised a hand toward the other D.I.'s and went out. He didn't go far, but turned into the detective sergeants' room nearby. Peel was one of half a dozen still there, and Peel looked almost as tired as Sloan.

"We're going home, Jim," Sloan said. "Come on."

"But—"

"Come on."

Peel shrugged, and picked up his hat, too. They went along the wide passages of the Yard without a word, then down in the lift, then out into the courtyard and the starry night. Traffic was thin on the Embankment; the sharp noise of a car horn sounded loud.

"Only we're not going to the home Chatworth told me to go to," Sloan said, as he opened the door of his car.

They got in.

"Where?" asked Peel, eagerly.

"Brammer's flat," Sloan said. "He's not officially missing and we can't get a search warrant, but I still want to go there. Ready to take a chance?"

"Hurry," Peel said.

12

Love from Ruth

Brammer lived in a small flat in a narrow street close to Covent Garden market. It was on two floors, the front door on the landing of the second floor of the building. The slightly sour smell of overripe fruit was wafted into the doorway and up the narrow staircase as Peel and Sloan walked up. They made plenty of noise. They passed a lighted doorway, and paused to listen, but heard no sound.

The landing outside Brammer's flat was in darkness.

Sloan switched on a torch. It showed on a brass letter box and knocker which needed polishing, and on varnish which had lost its shine, and on a doorbell.

Peel pressed this, but nothing happened. He pressed again, and knocked loudly. There was still no answer.

"I always said I'd make a good thief," he said, and grinned as he took a picklock out of his pocket. "Now all that has to happen is getting caught in the act. We'd be held on a charge of burglary or—"

"Get on with it." Sloan was edgy.

Peel grunted, and began to work on the lock. It was easy to open, and it soon clicked back. Silent darkness met them from inside the flat. Peel pushed the door open wider, and muttered:

"Anyone who has a lock as old as that ought to pay double insurance. A kid could force it."

"Let's get the door shut," Sloan said.

Peel closed the door.

They waited in the silence before switching on the torch; Peel found the light switch and pressed it down. They were in a small hallway. Doors led to the right and left, and just in front of them was another flight of wooden steps.

The room on the left was a little bit of everything. A divan in one corner was rumpled, as if someone had used it recently. There were two easy chairs and a small couch, a round table of polished mahogany which shone very brightly, and a pedestal desk in one corner. On this was a portable typewriter and a litter of papers—all the paraphernalia a man was likely to want when writing. Above it and on the nearby walls were bookshelves; in another corner was a baby grand piano. A recent photograph of Pauline Weston stood on that in a silver frame. The black-and-white coloring hardly did justice to her delicate complexion, but the candor and the calmness of the girl showed clearly.

There were letters from Hann-Gorlay and from the man who was giving him a lot of support in the Citizens' League organization—a Rodney Matthewson; all the letters were about some forthcoming meetings; Sloan glanced through these, as Peel sniffed.

"Fusty," he said. "Brammer hasn't been here for several days, that's certain."

"Nip upstairs and see what's doing," Sloan said.

Peel went, moving very quietly for a big man. Sloan began to search the desk, careful to leave everything as he found it. With a search warrant, he did a job like this every week of his life; without one, he felt as if he were committing a desperate crime.

He could hear Peel moving about in the room above, but there wasn't much noise. He finished his own search, and convinced himself that nothing here would help the quest for Roger.

Peel came downstairs.

"Anything?" he asked, and there was a casual note in his voice—a shade too casual.

"No—what have you found?" Sloan demanded.

"How about this?" asked Peel, and held out a photograph. "In a dressing-table drawer," he added.

It was a photograph of Ruth Linder, and across the bottom corner was a boldly written: *To Bram. With Love, Ruth.*

Sloan stood looking at it for some time. Peel fidgeted with cigarettes, but didn't light one.

"If Roger had found this he would have asked Brammer a lot of questions," Sloan said softly. "According to him, Brammer's always trying to convince him that Ruth is behind it all. This says that Brammer's been pretty good friends with the woman he's trying to fix. Film stars and prima donnas might give away signed photographs *ad lib*, but not the Ruth Linders of this world. Still, it isn't much." Disappointment echoed in his voice. "I'm losing my grip. I'd kidded myself that we'd find something worthwhile here. We can take it that Brammer's really missing." He gave a little shudder. "Every time I lift the telephone I think I'm going to be told that Roger's been found dead." He paused. "Let's get out of here."

Soon they were in the street, with two lamps spreading a little light, and the stars above. The sour smell was much more pronounced as they walked into the wind and toward Sloan's car.

A tall woman was standing near it wearing a loose-fitting coat of perfect cut. Not until she moved did Sloan recognize Pauline Weston.

"Is Bram back?" she said quietly.

"No."

"You aren't very much use, are you?" she said, and there was an undertone of irony in her voice. "You can't find either West or Bram."

She turned on her heel, and walked along the street. A man joined her near the corner.

"Find out who that is," Sloan ordered quickly.

Peel was already on the move.

Pauline and her companion made no attempt to evade him. It wasn't long before he recognized Charles Mortimer. Peel didn't speak, but watched them get into a taxi before going back to Sloan.

"It's Mortimer."

"I'd like to know what Ruth is playing at with him," Sloan said, and added peevishly, "We need two men for every one we've got, that's the hell of it."

They got into the car.

Janet West awoke, when it was still dark. She could not guess the time. The street lamps were on, and a man was walking steadily along the

110

pavement. Probably it was one of the two police-men on special duty in Bell Street.

There was no sound from the boys.

She turned over, desperation and despair heavy upon her. She knew that she wasn't likely to get off to sleep again. Her last thought before falling asleep had been of Roger; it was her first, now. Sleep seemed to bring no rest, no pausing in the flow of tormented anxiety—she was continually fearful; keyed up for a ring of the telephone and the news that Roger had been found dead.

Roger had been missing for three days now; three and a *half* days.

If she went to the shops, she sensed that the neighbors and tradesfolk were watching her and pointing her out. On a bus, it was the same. In the street, she dreaded the thought that she would be stopped by a neighbor with the kindly but so hurt-ful questions.

"Is there any news, Mrs. West?"

If she picked up a newspaper, she would see Roger's name in a headline on the front page. The first day the news had broken, it seemed to crowd everything else off the newspapers. The *Courier* had coupled it with the fact that Brammer had been missing for the same time—in fact for an hour or two longer, as far as it could be proved.

But the worst, by far the worst, was the silent waiting, the pathetic longing, of the boys.

On the first day they had burst out with ques-tions, and Janet had burst into tears. She hadn't realized what had happened to them then, but something significant had. Next time they came home from school they asked the questions only with their eyes. Now she could picture those eyes

111

—Richard's deep blue and huge, Martin's grave and steady and gray, asking, pleading:

"*Please*, Mum, is there any news?"

They didn't speak, and she didn't answer except by looking away from them.

There had been anxieties before; fears, too; and at times a feeling that Roger wouldn't come back. Never before had the boys been deeply affected. It told her that they were growing up, added to the torment, gave it almost unbearable poignancy.

She wasn't alone any more in being obsessed by fear. At school, in the streets and while playing, Richard and Martin felt the same.

She heard a car turn into the street.

Her heart almost stopped, and then began to thump. Why should a car pass along at this hour? —it was dark, pitch dark outside.

She sat up.

The car drew nearer. She felt as if she were being suffocated. *Could* it be Roger?

The car stopped.

She caught her breath, made herself fling the bedclothes to one side, and started to get out of bed.

"Who—" she heard a man say, and knew that it was one of the police in the street.

Next, she heard the shots. There were four of them, in quick succession. They roared out, blasting the silence. There was another choked cry and then unfamiliar noises. She thought she heard men falling.

She screamed.

She knew that it was mad to scream; part of her mind was telling her not to wake the boys, but she couldn't keep the scream back. She was moving all

112

the time, getting out of bed, stumbling toward the window.

The engine of the car snorted. As she neared the window, headlights blazed out. Looking out she caught a glimpse of a man on the pavement, lying flat; and of another in the road. It looked as if the car were going straight over this one. She saw something else, something which looked like a huge box, near the gate.

She was hysterical, and screamed again.

"No, no, no!"

Then there came a voice behind her.

"Mum, don't." It was Martin, desperate. "Mum, please don't, please."

She spun round, and ran toward him. He was sturdy and massive, and something to clutch tightly. She couldn't find words, but at least she didn't scream any more. She felt his arms go round her, and could hear the beating of his heart. There were other sounds, now, and she thought that she heard voices outside.

"Mum, what's the matter, what's happened?" Martin asked. "Is Dad—"

"No," she said hoarsely. "There was—shooting. Martin, what am I saying, there wasn't anything, I'm just—"

"Mum, please don't pretend," Martin said. "I'm old enough to know if anything awful's happened. Was there shooting?"

She could only just see him; he was ten years old; and he was in desperate earnest.

"Yes," she said. "I—I ought to ring 999, Scoopy darling, oughtn't I? I was so frightened, I hardly knew what I was doing, but I'm better now you're here."

113

She clung to him as he turned toward the telephone.

He lifted the receiver, dialed 999, knowing that was the Information Room at the Yard. He reported, quietly, that there had been shooting in Bell Street, Chelsea, outside the home of Chief Inspector West.

He put on the light.

By then voices sounded in the street; men's and women's. Martin went to the window. Janet felt she should stop him, but didn't feel that she could. He leaned out. Below, men were bending over the outstretched bodies, another was standing by the big crate. Words came floating up.

"Send for a doctor."

"I've told the police," Martin called out, very clearly. Everyone below looked round, startled. "They're bound to bring a doctor," he added.

Janet was close by Martin at the window, and visible against the light. That reassured the neighbors in the street. Someone came out of another house, nearby, and looked at the crate.

"Scoop, you must get your dressing gown," Janet said.

"Well, you ought to have yours on, too." Martin was quite matter-of-fact. "It's a quarter to six, Mum. Would you like a cup of tea?"

"I—yes, Scoop darling, I'd love one!"

"I'll just pop a kettle on," Martin said, and turned toward the door.

As he reached it, a man outside exclaimed:

"Look! There's a man in this crate—a body!"

13

The Crate

The relief from tension which Martin had brought disappeared at the words spoken in the street. Janet stood rigid, felt her color fleeing, coldness seizing her limbs. She saw Martin hesitate just outside the door. He stopped and turned.

"Sure?" a man asked from outside.

"Yes. Got a torch?"

"Mum," Martin said, very firmly, "I'm just going downstairs and see what I can do to help."

He didn't wait for an answer, but turned and hurried off. All Janet's instinct was to call out, "No! Come back!" but she couldn't find the words. Martin disappeared, while men in the street muttered.

Janet was sure of the truth; and believed that Martin had sensed it. There was a man in the crate which had been dumped outside this house; why dump the crate here, if it weren't Roger?

Janet moved toward the window. She didn't want to look out, yet knew that she had to. As she reached it, she saw Martin running into the street while two men shone torches onto the wooden crate. Then Martin drew level with them, and peered between the boards.

Two cars turned into Bell Street, one from each end, and each had headlights shining. These were the patrol cars answering Martin's summons. Their engines were loud, and yet they seemed not to break the silence.

There were the wounded, perhaps the dead or dying policemen and other neighbors and the two by Martin—and all of them were looking toward Martin. Janet was, too. He had peered between the boards, and then slowly backed away. Janet couldn't see his face, but could see the reaction of the others, who watched him.

It was as if they were struck dumb.

Then Martin raised his head, and looked at Janet.

Perhaps it was a trick of the light, due to the brilliance of the headlamps; whatever the cause, he seemed to be sending her a message, a desperate: *"It's happened, it's happened, I'll look after you"* kind of message.

Then the police cars stopped and hurried out. The tableau was broken. Voices sounded normal again.

"What is it?"

"Who's hurt?"

"Two men, shot."

"Two?"

"Did anyone see—"

"And there's Chief Inspector West."

"Did anyone see—" A pause. *"What?"*

"Chief Inspector West, in that crate."

"Good—God!"

Silence fell again, on everyone. It was only for a second, but it existed. Martin broke it, very clearly.

"Please," he said, "will someone let my father out?"

One of the police from a patrol car had the sense to think about Janet. He came hurrying upstairs with Martin. Bursting with a sudden frenzy of anxiety to get downstairs, Janet met them on the landing, fumbling with the sash of her dressing gown.

"Sure you ought to come outside, Mrs. West?" The policeman took her arm firmly.

"Of course!"

"All right—don't trip up," the man said. His calmness was like a douche of cold water. "Take it easy. You go first, nipper—you're Martin, aren't you? Call you Scoop or something, don't they?" The gruff voice was like a steady hand.

A brawny arm went round Janet's waist. They got to the hall, and Martin hesitated, then went boldly forward. A rending sound outside told that the boards of the crate were being prized open.

Janet could see only that. The police cars, the ambulances which had arrived, the crowd which was growing thicker every moment, the neighbors —all those things meant nothing. There were two uniformed police prizing up the wooden staves— and doubled up inside the crate was Roger. Janet could just see that it was a man.

The man's hold on her waist was very tight. She looked around desperately for Martin, and saw that the patrolman's other arm was round the boy's shoulder.

"Easy," one of the policemen said.

"Mind his face."

Nails creaked out of the soft wood.

Another man moved toward them, shorter, in plain clothes, and carrying a small bag. Janet didn't recognize him, but someone said "doctor." She held her breath. She didn't quite realize when it happened, but suddenly Martin's hand was in hers; then he pressed close against her, frightened. A woman from one of the nearby houses came and joined them.

The patrolman lit a cigarette, then coughed.

The two men stretched Roger out on the pavement as they would a corpse.

Martin's fingers seemed to cut into Janet's hand.

The doctor bent over Roger, hiding his face. Janet moved forward, very slowly. In her heart she was quite sure what had happened—that Roger was dead. She knew that somehow she had to steel herself into looking into his expressionless face.

The doctor straightened up.

"Get him to bed—get him warm." He swung round. "He's alive, Mrs. West."

Janet fainted.

"Get busy," the Yard C.I. said when he reached Bell Street. "Check that crate for prints, find where it was made, search every timber yard and wood factory in London. After that—"

His voice went on and on.

It was six o'clock on the following afternoon.

Janet brushed a wisp of hair from her forehead, as she heard the telephone. She was in the kitchen, getting the boys' tea-cum-supper ready. They weren't yet home. A young policeman moved from the hall into the front room to answer the tele-

118

phone. Janet listened. She was slightly flushed from the heat of the kitchen, but looked relaxed and rested. She had slept from eight o'clock until three this afternoon—from the moment she had been assured that Roger would soon come round.

Roger was known to have been drugged, but nothing suggested that the dose would be lethal.

He was upstairs now, sleeping almost naturally, nearly free from the drug's hold. Except for a few hypodermic needle punctures in his arm, a surface cut on the back of his neck and a bruise or two on his head, there was nothing the matter with him.

The policeman appeared.

"It's for you, Mrs. West."

"Oh, thanks." Janet wiped her hands on a tea towel, and hurried into the front room. "Who is it?"

"A lady, ma'am."

"Oh. Hallo? . . . This is Janet West speaking."

"Good afternoon, Mrs. West," a woman said. She had a deep, pleasing voice. "I'm so anxious to hear how Chief Inspector West is."

"Much better, thank you. Who is that?" The voice was just a voice to Janet, and yet she felt that it was one which she would find it easy to remember.

"This is Ruth Linder," the woman said.

"Ruth—*Linder*."

The woman laughed—as if the surprise in Janet's voice amused her.

"Yes," she said. "You will tell the chief inspector that I was inquiring, won't you? And I wonder if you will tell him that I'd like to see him as soon as he's well enough to get about."

"I will," Janet said.

"I *may* be able to help him."

"You're very kind."

"Not at all, Mrs. West. I'm so glad he's better. Good-by."

"Good-by," echoed Janet.

She was preoccupied when she went back to the kitchen. She knew what Roger thought about Ruth Linder; knew that he would be astonished at this show of interest. Perhaps the best thing would be to telephone Sloan, at the Yard.

Sloan and Peel had looked in, and had been absurdly like children, delighted at what had happened. Chatworth had also been here. In some odd way, it was as if until they actually saw him, none of them would believe that Roger was back.

Janet telephoned Sloan, but he wasn't there; so she left a message. Then she began to lay the table. It was now a quarter past six. It wouldn't be long before the boys came rushing in, and burst out with a torrent of questions: that awful silence would be gone.

As soon as Roger came round, she was to telephone the yard.

She heard a tapping on the ceiling.

She dropped everything, sending a knife clattering to the floor, and raced upstairs. The constable watched her, grinning. The bedroom door was ajar, and she thrust it wide.

Roger was sitting up in bed.

He looked pale and dazed—but not bemused. He recognized her. He saw her move toward him, and must have realized in a flash how she was feeling, what had been happening here.

Janet felt his arms go round her, and then tighten, viselike. It was a moment of ecstasy; of exaltation.

120

At last, she drew back.

Roger looked up at her for a long time. Then deliberately took the edge of the sheet and wiped the tears from her eyes. They didn't speak. The silence went on for a long time, dear and precious, until Roger said huskily:

"How long have I been away?"

"Darling!"

"Honestly, I don't know."

"But—"

"I swear I don't know," he said.

"Nearly four days," Janet choked.

"Four—days," Roger echoed.

As they stared at each other, the boys rushed in at the front door, the policeman spoke to them, and they came hurrying upstairs, obviously on tiptoe, and whispering excitedly.

Within fifteen minutes the Yard was sending men to the side street off Blackfriars Bridge Road, trying to check back to the time of Roger's disappearance. Calls went out throughout London and Home Counties areas for small, red Morris Minors.

"Check 'em all, question everyone, hold anyone who hasn't a clear alibi," Sloan ordered.

At Bell Street, Roger was told by the doctor that he would need two or three days to recover from the doping. But he was already beginning to fret, and was up but not dressed when Sloan and Peel came to see him. He'd had a meal, and was pulling on a cigarette. Even the sight of the rejoicing Yard men did him good.

He talked....

"And you just don't remember a thing," Sloan said.

"That's the simple truth," said Roger. "They knocked me out when I turned into the side street. Since then I haven't been conscious for a minute until today."

"Crazy," said Peel.

"Don't blame me!"

"I mean, they are. Why should they—" Peel broke off.

"Judging from the number of punctures in my arm, I've had a shot of morphia three times each day," Roger said. "So they meant to keep me under. But why let me go free? Why not treat me as they have the rest?" He drew hard at his cigarette. "I know, I know; we shan't find the answer to that until we know all the answers. All right. I don't know a thing that's happened over the last four days, Bill—tell me what's been cooking."

Sloan talked; Roger listened and smoked.

There had been several attacks on the police, all by unnamed youths, but only one shooting outbreak: that in Bell Street. One policeman had been killed, the other hadn't yet recovered consciousness, and there was real risk that he wouldn't live.

Robbery with violence was becoming rife all over the country, with London the worst spot.

Nothing had been learned from the packing case in which Roger had been "delivered." No one yet knew where it had been made. An early morning cyclist had been found who had seen a small van turn into Bell Street, about the time of the shooting. Tire prints on the road hadn't helped.

There had been no more warnings.

The newspaper campaign was hotter than it had ever been, and with Brammer missing, the *Courier* was screeching even more loudly than ever.

The Wimbledon meeting, over which the solicitor Matthewson had presided and which Hann-Gorlay had addressed, had been crowded. Five hundred local residents, with only one or two dissentients, voted for arms for the police and harsh reprisals on all the violent criminals caught. There had been several other meetings in and near London, with Hann-Gorlay the chief speaker and the same Rodney Matthewson in the chair.

"Hann-Gorlay's good, by all accounts, and Matthewson brilliant in a dry way. He's a shrewd lawyer, and keeps well on the right side of us," Sloan explained. "But there's a lot of talk of a corps of vigilantes."

"Armed?" Roger asked sharply.

"No one's said so, but I can't see a volunteer force like that going about without weapons of some kind."

"The bloody fools," Roger growled.

"Listen, Roger," Sloan said; "are you so sure? We *are* short of men, and a kind of peacetime Home Guard—"

"Now look here, don't you fall for that line of argument," Roger said gruffly. "Give us armed vigilantes and armed police, and every young desperado in London will get hold of a gun somehow. If you oppose violence with violence you get more violence."

Sloan said, "Don't forget that several of our chaps were murdered in cold blood." His voice was rather cool; for once he wasn't seeing eye to eye with Roger.

Roger slid into a different subject.

"Brammer's not back, you say?"

Sloan seemed glad to switch the conversation.

"No sign or sound." He scratched his nose, then took a long look at Peel. "As you're still off duty, Roger, you can hear about this. Two idiots broke into Brammer's flat a couple of nights ago. They found that he had a signed photograph of Ruth Linder—signed with her love. It was probably taken just before her present Society Beauty act. They found nothing else which might have involved Brammer in this."

Roger said softly, "So Brammer knew Ruth pretty well. You heard about her kind inquiries after me, didn't you?"

"Yes."

"I think I might go and see what she wanted to see me about," Roger said. "That's my first job." He lit a cigarette. "I wish to hell I could get rid of the idea that it's all a hideous hoax. I feel as if she's simply making a fool of me, that someone is just out to make the Yard a laughingstock. Think what fun I've given them. They kidnap me, then send me back like a carcass, as if to say that it wasn't worth keeping me—or even worth killing me."

Peel grinned.

"One way of insulting you—leaving you alive because they weren't scared of you!"

"That's it."

"It's hideous all right," Sloan said. "But it's no hoax. They've got some reason for it, and don't tell me it's a vendetta, I won't buy that one either."

They looked hard at one another; Roger knew that Sloan disagreed with him strongly about arming the police, although he'd only said so by implication. Sloan was mad at the crooks; perhaps mad enough to have his judgment warped.

The telephone bell rang, and Sloan answered.

The Yard was calling. As he listened, his expression told Roger and Peel that this was news.

"Yes," he said into the telephone, "watch 'em both." He rang off, and turned round. "Brammer's back," he said. "He's just arrived at Wilmington Place—to see Ruth Linder. What wouldn't I give to be able to hear what they're talking about!"

They saw Brammer a few hours afterward. He looked like a walking corpse. His story was the same as Roger's, and he had exactly the same number of needle pricks—fourteen.

He had been propped up against the doorway of his own flat; no one had seen who had brought him home.

The *Courier* really went to town.

14

Invitation

Roger pulled his car up outside the block of flats in Wilmington Place. The Yard man watching had given him an almost imperceptible salute as he'd passed—and by staying where he was, at the street corner, made it plain that he had nothing to report.

The sun was warm.

It was nearly eleven o'clock, on Roger's third morning back at Bell Street, and his first morning officially on duty. He didn't feel at his brightest, but didn't feel too bad. Unless he exerted himself too much, he would be all right.

A lift boy took him up to Ruth Linder's flat.

He hadn't been here before, but knew that the flats had a reputation for luxury and ostentation. The reputation was justified. There were gilt mirrors, deep-piled carpets, everything that unexacting millionaires might expect.

Roger rang the bell.

He was still puzzled by Ruth Linder, but that was only part of his worry. Four days in his life were missing; he hadn't any idea where he had been, knew what had happened to him only by what the doctors and his own common sense could tell him. The four blank days harassed him much more than he had expected.

There was much more than that, too. There were the murders; and there was the campaign. Except for the almost inevitable robberies with violence, nothing had happened since he had come round; but he knew that in every police station in London there was an air of expectancy, almost of fearful expectancy.

The door of the flat opened. A trim maid looked up into Roger's face and smiled. She was not only trim, she was pretty.

"Chief Inspector West?"

"Yes."

"Please come in; Miss Ruth is expecting you."

"Miss Ruth"—spoken as if this were a family servant. Old Benny's adopted niece had certainly found the way to make it look as if she had been born to riches.

The apartment was not so ostentatious as the passages and the hall. It was large and spacious, quietly and pleasantly decorated, with pastel blues and green predominating.

The maid opened a door on the right of the front door, tapped and said:

"Chief Inspector West, Miss Ruth."

Ruth stood up from a couch in the window— and Brammer stood up from an armchair in the corner.

It was Ruth who caught and held the eye; a bold, vital beauty, dressed to emphasize every line of her figure, lips glistening red. Voluptuous was only a word.

127

Brammer, with his dark, restless eyes and his hooked nose and thick, thrusting lips, had an almost satyrish look.

Roger glanced at him, then back to the girl.

"I'm very glad you've come," Ruth said, smoothly. "As soon as I knew when you were coming, I asked Mr. Brammer if he'd be present, too. But sit down, please. Will you have a drink?"

"No, thanks."

"Coffee—or tea?"

"Well—coffee."

She pressed a bell push near the fireplace. The maid came in, and Ruth ordered coffee, while Brammer dropped back into his chair and glowered. Here was Beauty and the Beast, new version. In Brammer's room there was a photograph of Beauty, signed with her love.

The maid went out.

"You see," said Ruth to Roger, "I think we should be very frank with each other, Chief Inspector. I know that Bram here has been suggesting to you that I am actually responsible for this—ah—campaign."

Her eyes seemed to ridicule the very thought.

Roger said dryly, "Are you?"

She laughed.

"I want to tell you that I think *he* is," she said.

Brammer didn't move. He was sitting back with the tips of his fingers pressed together and his long legs stretched out, looking at Ruth without any expression.

The room was very quiet.

"She's fooling you, Handsome," Brammer said at last. "She hates the pair of us—you because you put her Uncle Benny inside, me because I did the story on her father before he was hanged. I guarantee that this case will prove that murder can be hereditary." His voice had the lash of anger, although it was quiet and almost drawling. "Don't make any mistake, Handsome—she means to make monkeys out of both of us."

"How difficult," murmured Ruth, "with Chief Inspector West!" Her gaze mocked Brammer. "I've discovered something about Bram, Chief Inspector."

"At one time and another I've discovered a lot about both of you," Roger said mildly.

Ruth laughed.

"I'm sure you have. But have you discovered that he is insane? Fanaticism *is* a form of insanity, isn't it? He is, you know. It's because he has always hated violence. I don't quite know how it began, but I do know that the one thing that can make him violent is violence!" Her eyes did all the laughing for her. "He rages and froths at the mouth because of it. He is absolutely beside himself with rage because of the violence of all these young criminals. He doesn't think the police can find the answer to the crimes—as things are. He thinks that the one answer to crimes of violence *is* violence. You know how passionately he's pleaded for arms for the police, don't you? How he's worked up this campaign. He says that it's the newspaper's fault, but he's really behind it. It's boosting circulation very well, so the management doesn't object."

There was a tap at the door; the maid came in with coffee. The room was silent until she had gone out again.

"What I'm saying," Ruth went on with soft insistence, "is that this hatred of crime with violence has driven Bram mad. He thinks I'm responsible for some of it. In fact *he* is—he's instigated this campaign to force the hand of the authorities. He thinks they're bound to arm all the police, and to introduce much more vicious punishment. Don't you, Bram?"

It was difficult to guess what Brammer thought. He looked at her with his hooded eyes half closed, and his thick lips parted slightly. His teeth just showed. It came to Roger that few men would ever look more evil. Give Brammer a pair of horns, and he could be the Devil himself.

"No," he said, "I don't. Don't let her fool you, Handsome. She always hated the police because of her parents, and it's turned her mind. She's clever. It wouldn't matter what game she started, she would go a long way in it. The trouble is, she's turned bad. A bad woman is ten times worse than a bad man, or don't you need telling that?"

Roger was watching Ruth.

She had *enjoyed* accusing Brammer. She was enjoying all of this.

She turned to Roger.

"Now you just have to take your choice, Chief Inspector," she said sweetly.

Roger said, "Why do you two hate each other?"

Neither spoke.

"Bram," Roger went on, "I had a phone call, supposed to be from you, saying that you had something to show me. As a result, I was held up outside the *Courier* office. Did you telephone?"

"No." Brammer's eyes opened a shade wider.

"You disappeared at the same time as I did.

What were you doing just before you were picked up?"

"I was trying to find proof that Ruth is behind all this killing, supplying the weapons, encouraging the kids, buying the stuff they steal."

"And you didn't get it," Ruth mocked.

"There's time," said Brammer.

"Ruth," Roger said mildly, and tried to make sure that he could see both their faces at the same time, to judge the reactions, "how long were you in love with Bram, and why did you break things off?"

She looked astounded.

Bram made an odd little noise in the back of his throat, and then began to grin. He looked grotesquely satyrish as he shrugged his coat into position, then moved across to Ruth.

"We can't keep any secrets from the police, you see," he said. "Why don't you tell him?"

He turned away, and went out. He didn't slam the door, but closed it gently. But the outer door slammed. The girl stood and watched the closed door as if she could think only of Brammer, and hardly realized that Roger was present.

"Very clever," she said at last. "Can't a woman make a mistake? Dear Bram. What a swine he is."

Roger gave her time to go on, but she had finished. So he asked:

"What makes you say that?"

"Just my knowledge of Bram." That was almost a sneer.

"Why did you want to see me?" Roger asked abruptly.

"I wanted to tell you that it's Brammer."

"The police are unreasonable people. They need proof before they can take any action."

"Watch his girl friend, Pauline Weston," Ruth said softly. "She has a lot of money, seldom does any work, is supposed to be an analytical chemist. She has a lot of young boy friends, too, including Charles Mortimer. I'm not sure that Mortimer didn't fool both of us."

Roger didn't speak, just watched Ruth. She smiled at him, tight-lipped. Then she thawed, drew near, seemed to will him to dwell upon her beauty. But a bell rang faintly and there were sounds in the hall. The door opened, and a youthful-looking man appeared—dark-haired, handsome in a dashing way; immaculately dressed.

Ruth's expression changed. She looked radiantly young as she moved forward eagerly.

"Hallo, darling! I didn't expect you so soon. Do you know Chief Inspector West? Inspector, this is Sir Neville Hann-Gorlay."

The men murmured "how-do's" but Roger didn't stay long—just long enough to feel pretty sure that Hann-Gorley was in love with Ruth; that the man worshiped her.

Was Ruth making fools of them both?

Brammer had said that Ruth would do everything she could to hurt Pauline. He was probably right. Apparently Ruth hadn't known that the police were watching Pauline as closely as they were watching her and the Aldgate shop.

In fact, Peel's special job was to watch Pauline.

On the afternoon that Roger had met Hann-Gorlay, Peel called the office with excitement in his voice, and Peel didn't get excited easily.

"All right, take it easy," Roger said. "The Weston girl hasn't taken a powder, has she?"

"Not yet," Peel crowed, "but she probably will. Know what I've found out? She had a red Morris Minor. A scarlet last year's model. Now it's black."

"What?"

"It was red, now it's black," Peel repeated, still crowing. "It was red until the day you were shanghaied, Handsome." In his excitement he forgot that he was talking to and not about Roger. "Then it went in for a bashed wing, and she decided to have it black. Said red showed up the dirt too much, or some nonsense."

"I think I'll come and have a look at it," Roger said.

The car was at a small garage near Pauline's flat. Peel, still cock-a-hoop, didn't think that the girl knew that he was interested in it. He was actually on his back, looking up at the front part of the engine when Roger arrived, and he scrambled up.

"It's had false number plates on in its time," he announced. "The garage chap says he didn't know—"

"And what's more, the garage chap damned well didn't know," growled a man who had approached from the two cream-painted petrol pumps, wiping his hands on a rag. "I'm the chap, and I know what I'm talking about."

"Ever had it up on the hoist for servicing?" Roger asked amiably.

"Yes—several times."

"And you didn't notice a false number plate fitting?"

"Hell, no," the garage man said. He was a moody-looking forty, his stubble was turning gray

133

and he had a big bald patch. "Why should I? Anyhow, Miss Weston probably doesn't know, either. Too generous by half, that young woman. I know it's a good fault but it's still a fault."

Peel looked startled.

"How generous?" asked Roger, and offered cigarettes.

"Ta. Well, always letting other people borrow her car," the man said. "Young fools who knock the guts out of the engine if ever they get a chance. You'd think she'd have more sense, too, she's obviously a cut above them."

"You don't happen to know their names, do you?" Roger asked.

The garage man knew the name of only one man who occasionally borrowed Pauline's Morris Minor. It was Charles Mortimer, and the description fitted.

"That's fine," Roger said. "Now keep mum, will you? We're not after Miss Weston, but one of her boy friends. If you tell her about this, they'll be warned."

"I won't talk," the man promised.

"Does that mean you're not going to tackle the Weston girl?" asked Peel, as they went off. His manner was much more subdued.

"Not yet," Roger said. "Keep after her."

Pauline Weston saw Charles Mortimer most days, as well as several other youths in his circle. She saw Brammer as often as ever. Twice she was seen with small, dapper, middle-aged Rodney Matthewson. Matthewson became more and more prominent in organizing the Citizens' League meetings and his name was continually in the public eye. So far the League had done nothing to which the police could take exception, although each meeting was watched and closely reported on. Leaders like Matthewson and Hann-Gorlay were screened; all came through the tests easily.

Pauline was taking some part in the League's activities, possibly to help Brammer. It gave her an excuse to be at his office a great deal. This office had become a sort of unofficial H.Q. of the League, which had the *Courier*'s full support.

Pauline was still calm, poised, mature—and did nothing which gave Roger any excuse to take action. She used her newly painted car freely; so did Mortimer and two other youths. Roger made sure that they all had an alibi for the Fleet Street kidnapping, and still held off Pauline.

The prevailing tension served one good purpose; every Divisional man and every man at the Yard put a little more keenness into routine, and the temptation to let a thing go by default was killed stone dead. It was routine, not any particular discovery, which focused attention more squarely on Charles Mortimer.

He had been an acquaintance of Neil Harrock and of Prescott. He knew Ruth as well as any one of her friends, and was well acquainted with many of these. He paid Pauline Weston a lot of attention, although in some ways she kept him at arm's length; was friendly without being affectionate.

Son of a regular Army officer who had been killed early in the war, Mortimer had a good National Service record, but the deeper Roger probed, the more one fact emerged: there was a streak of viciousness in the man. And he had always been tense and edgy, thirsting—lusting—

for excitement. He was a good shot, but in some ways erratic and inclined to be surly and sullen. He lived in two furnished rooms which he rented near Kensington High Street, had enough money to live on, was never in debt. He gambled heavily, and seemed to win often.

"Find his bookmaker," Roger said. "Let's make sure that the money he gets comes from picking winners."

It wasn't easy at first, for Mortimer used different bookmakers. One named Micky Lamb, who ran a secondhand shop in Chelsea, said that Mortimer had the luck of the Devil, especially in picking doubles. It looked all right, but in the probing, one thing was established.

Charles Mortimer had no alibi for the night of Prescott's murder at the hospital.

"Keep checking," Roger urged Sloan. "Mortimer knows we're after him, but never mind. Just watch him. He's a hot-eyed, hot-blooded young brute. If you corner him, be careful."

15

Mass Meeting

For a week there was a period of uneasy calm. Several coshing attacks were made in different parts of the country, mostly in London. A policeman who interrupted two youths breaking into a shop in Croydon was attacked and left battered and unconscious but not seriously injured; the youths were found. There were no more letters, but silence brought no marked easing of the tension at the Yard or at the Divisions. Plans for double patrols in certain districts were put in hand, but most of the attacks had been made in supposedly "safe" districts, not in the notoriously bad areas.

Citizens' League branches had caught on, and were being formed in dozens of London districts, all pledged to work for an armed police force, doubled strength and violent punishment for cases of proved violence.

Members of Parliament were flooded with letters from constituents, many prominent people gave their names to the League, several retired judges gave it active support. Matthewson and Hann-Gorlay found themselves public figures.

With help from all the newspapers, the Movement became gigantic almost overnight.

None of this helped Roger or the Yard to track down the killer youths. None of it eased the present tension among the police. Mortimer, Ruth and Pauline Weston were watched with almost nervous thoroughness.

Still nothing that Pauline Weston did gave the police grounds for suspecting that she knew more than she should. Except Mortimer, the Yard found no connection between any of her friends and Ruth Linder's. She seemed to get more friendly with Mortimer than ever, but was more often with Brammer.

Roger was driving along Fleet Street when he saw them, three days after Ruth had named Pauline. A traffic block held him up. He pulled in to the curb and got out. Then he saw another man with them—small, dapper, middle-aged.

All three stopped.

"You don't know Mr. Rodney Matthewson, do you?" Brammer asked Roger. "Chief Inspector West, Rodney—"

Roger liked the lawyer's manner and firm handclasp; and the humor which lurked in his eyes.

"Now what are you plotting?" Roger demanded.

"We're really going to get you fellows looked after," Brammer said. "Arms and—"

"Did it ever occur to you that we might not want to carry guns?" Roger's voice sharpened.

Matthewson murmured, "But if we get this recruiting campaign and double your forces, as well as harsher punishment for the criminals, won't you be grateful?"

Roger said, "The gibbet didn't stop highway robbery—didn't anyone ever tell you that?"

"For a policeman," Matthewson observed, "you are remarkably humanitarian. However, I cannot believe that many of your colleagues would oppose sterner punishment. Be honest—would they?"

"No," Roger said grudgingly. "Not many." He thought of Sloan.

"That's what I like about Mr. West," said Pauline; "you can believe anything that he says."

She looked lovelier, Roger thought—but she still wasn't a beauty. Yet there was something right about her being with Brammer—nothing right about her seeing so much of Mortimer.

"Don't pay him too many compliments," Brammer said. "And let's answer his question—we're plotting the biggest demonstration yet, Handsome. In the Albert Hall...."

Two days later the *Courier* carried an editorial in support of a large advertisement, which read:

Anti "Terror" Campaign
MASS MEETING
in
ALBERT HALL

Chairman: Rodney Matthewson, Esq.
Speakers: Sir Neville Hann-Gorlay, M.P.
           Percival Smythe, O.B.E., M.P.
Tuesday........at 7:30 p.m.

Following the meetings in Chiswick, Golders Green, Wimbledon, Tottenham and other London boroughs, the *Courier* and the Campaign Committee have hired London's famous Albert Hall for a mass meeting which will demand:

ARMS FOR THE POLICE

A NATION-WIDE RECRUITING CAMPAIGN
PUNISHMENT TO FIT THE CRIMES

This Wave of Brutality Must Be Crushed

Roger himself went to a meeting in Hammersmith; Matthewson was the ideal chairman, Hann-Gorlay a brilliant speaker. The audience of over a thousand people was wildly enthusiastic.

Other newspapers carried the Albert Hall advertisement; if they could be believed, applications for tickets passed the half-million mark within three days.

Roger telephoned Brammer.

"I want three tickets for the meeting, Bram."

"I saw you at the Hammersmith show the other night," Brammer said. "Hann-Gorlay's good, isn't he? And our chairman isn't so bad, either. But don't let Ruth's friendship with Hann-Gorlay fool you." Roger could imagine Brammer's grin. "She's bad." Brammer paused. "Sure, I'll send the tickets. You'll have quite a time."

"I'll tell you someone else who'll have quite a time—that's the uniformed branch," Roger said. "We'll have to draft hundreds of extra police and hundreds of special constables to look after the meeting. They can only do it by taking men off the beat. If there's an outbreak of crime that night, you'll have yourselves to blame."

"One night won't make any difference," Brammer said. "If we can knock some sense into the heads of the Home Office, it'll be worth it."

Roger drafted plain-clothes men into the Hall for the night, and others in the streets. Everyone at the Yard felt uneasy, without being able to say why.

It was a fine, clear night.

According to reports which came from uniformed branches, the crowds heading toward the Albert Hall were thick by half-past four—for the meeting due to start at seven-thirty. By six o'clock the crowds were vast. Mounted police, standing by, moved in to help control. Smaller open-air meetings quickly sprang up in Kensington Gardens, near the Albert Memorial. The pavements about the circular walls of the Albert Hall itself were jammed with people, some with tickets, some without.

Ambulances were called to deal with fainting women and some who were injured in the crush.

Beyond the Albert Hall area every available policeman in London was on duty in the streets. The possibility that the lull in the attacks would come to an abrupt end that night was in the minds of many besides Roger.

At seven he arrived at the Hall with Sloan and Chatworth. Peel was in another part of the hall. Chatworth had to force his way through the crowd, both inside and out. He went ahead like a burly bull terrier, as if defying Roger and Sloan to make his path easier for him.

It took them nearly half an hour to reach their

seats. These were opposite the platform, where a single row of empty seats and a table were ready for the chairman and the speakers.

There was hubbub in the enormous, circular Hall, and hardly room to squeeze in another man. A great mass of faces, reaching almost as high as the roof, was turned toward the platform. Men seemed to outnumber women by three or four to one; and most of the men were youngish.

Chatworth pulled at a small cigar and glared about him. Roger sat back, feeling much more on edge than he let himself look. He was glad his gun was in his pocket.

A little file of men and women came onto the platform. Matthewson led the way, almost bald, very confident; the crowd jumped to its feet and began to cheer. The roar of applause as the speakers filed on filled the great dome as with thunder. It didn't stop when they sat down.

Chatworth just glowered about him. Roger watched—and didn't like much of what he saw. There was something here which went very deep. It was a note of anger—passionate anger, rage. These people were out for blood. This wasn't just a mass meeting, to protest; it went much further.

"I wouldn't like this mob to get out of control," Sloan whispered.

Chatworth growled, "What's that?"

"Nothing, sir."

Chatworth glared.

Roger was watching, as the roar of applause began to fade. Four men and two women were on the platform. Matthewson was in the chair. Next to him, on his right, was Neville Hann-Gorlay. The

142

potlight was already on him; he looked impres-
ively handsome, immaculately dressed.

Ruth Linder sat next to him.

Sloan nudged Roger.

"See her?"

"Yes. That's the first time she's come into the
pen with him," Roger said.

"Who's the chairman?" Chatworth demanded,
lthough he knew quite well.

"Rodney Matthewson, chairman of the Citizens'
League," Roger told him. "He's good."

"They're five minutes late," Chatworth snapped.

Almost on his words, Matthewson stood up, to
nother roar of applause. He stopped it with a
mile and a self-deprecatory wave of his hands. As
t died down, all but a few lights went out. The
potlight was on the chairman.

"Theatrical nonsense," growled Chatworth.

Two or three people near him glowered, one
man moved as if to touch his shoulder. Chatworth
took no notice, but watched Matthewson.

As soon as he began to speak, the little man became much more impressive. He had a deep,
pleasant voice, and didn't make the mistake of
being too solemn. He was very glad to see so many
people present, sorry only that so many others
hadn't been able to get in. It showed a proper understanding of the gravity of the situation, and he
hoped that it would impress those in authority,
and make them understand how the people felt.
That was, if those in authority realized that there
were such things as people....

He said that with a little quirk of a smile. It was
easy, almost cheap—but it won the crowd.

"All the newspapers which have sponsored this

143

meeting—and I may say will sponsor many others"—he had to pause for a roar of applause—"deserve our warm gratitude. I shall not name any one of them, as each is now giving unstinted support. I shall remind you during the meeting that there are handbills available in the foyers and in the exit lobbies, and I suggest that each of you takes enough home to distribute, say in his or her street. We should be able to cover the whole of London that way—and even leave a few to spare for those gentlemen at the Home Office."

The laughter which followed wasn't really of amusement. It had an ugly ring.

A note was slipped into Roger's hand. He opened it, and read:

Pauline Weston is in the Hall

He passed the note to Sloan, who nodded. Chatworth noticed nothing, was intent on the chairman. Roger kept looking at the Yard men, recognizing a few of them near at hand. Brammer was at the Press table, in front of the speakers.

Uniformed police or special constables were at all the doorways.

"It is our intention," Matthewson was saying, "to seek the strongest possible support for this campaign to wipe out the wave of terror in this great city—in this great country. But I will not trespass on the time or the subject of my friend Sir Neville Hann-Gorlay, Member of Parliament for..."

His last words were drowned in the roar of cheering.

Hann-Gorlay stood up with an air. He glanced down at Ruth, and she smiled up at him. Anyone who saw her face, caught as it was in the circle of the spotlight, must have been struck by her beauty. It was almost as if Hann-Gorlay depended on her for support.

Hann-Gorlay stepped forward.

There was a quality of magic in his voice and his manner. Here was an orator who could sway tens of thousands. His words were simple and effective, and in a few seconds he won complete mastery. The words were comparatively unimportant; the nuance that he gave them, the subtle emphasis, breathed life into them all.

"...And let us not forget those who suffer from these brutal attacks. It is one thing to be charitable, to forgive those who sin, to treat these *devils* as if they were invalids to be pitied. It is another to forget the plight of a woman robbed of her man—a child robbed of the guidance and the sanctuary of a father....

"...I could tell you harrowing stories of men and women, once in good health, with a glowing future before them, and a wife or husband and family with whom to share it—men and women who could laugh, as you have laughed tonight. I have seen them after young brutes had coshed the very sense out of them. Hale, hearty men—suddenly half paralyzed. Intelligent men turned into idiots. Old folk viciously attacked in the evening of their lives. Young folk wickedly attacked so that not only their bodies have been affected, but through all their years they will remember with horror the blows which came out of the darkness."

There was hardly a movement, hardly a sound but the one man's voice, in the great hall.

"Now what is it that we ask?" Hann-Gorlay went

on. "Simply protection for our wives, our children and ourselves. That is the simple duty of the State, that—"

The applause burst upon him like a torrent, nothing he could do could stop it. He waited, pale-faced, looking very tense; and there was tension in Ruth, too. Watching, listening, Roger felt that Hann-Gorlay was almost in a trance; believed passionately in everything that he said.

The roar died away, and he went on:

"Is it too much to ask that these armed beasts should be met with arms? Force with force? . . . Are we to continue to stand by and watch our policemen—our loyal, faithful, courageous friends in blue—*slaughtered?* Are we . . ."

The wave of applause drowned his words, men were jumping to their feet, cheering.

"Give these men arms, and they will be able to defend themselves as well as us—they will be able to protect our property. But we want more. Where there is one policeman today, unarmed, we want two tomorrow—fully armed . . ."

He had to wait again for silence.

"And we call for a recruiting campaign which we know will be answered magnificently when the people realize that at last the authorities—the government—is ready to tackle this awful problem with all the vigor that an emergency demands."

He had the crowd where he wanted it; won silence or cheers, shrill laughter or tense grins; they gave him everything he called for.

His voice grew more powerful, he seemed to grow bigger, he commanded a great silence as he cried:

"It was said long ago, and well said, that there should be an eye for an eye, a tooth for a tooth, a life for a life. That is our demand tonight. Let us use the cat-o'-nine tails, let us bring back harsh, let us have *terrible* punishment inflicted upon those who are guilty of the brutal crimes. If any man kills, he is hanged. Why should he not suffer, in kind, if he makes others suffer in other ways? It will be the greatest deterrent—"

The crack of a shot, the flash of a gun, broke across his words.

16

Mob Law

After the shot, there was silence.

It lasted only for a moment: a shocked moment when there was no sound at all. It was as if every man and woman in the hall had stopped breathing.

Then came a roar which was much louder than anything that had come before; a roar which held a note of ferocity.

Hann-Gorlay, upright until that moment, leaned across the table in front of him. Matthewson jumped up, and Ruth Linder was at their side in a flash. But they couldn't save Hann-Gorlay from falling; he slumped over the table as others rushed to help; then he fell.

Brammer from the Press table was on the move at once.

Roger jumped on his feet, saying sharply:

"Come on, Bill. You stay there, Sir Guy."

He began to move down the gangway, with Sloan just behind him. Chatworth ignored his advice, and followed. Not far off, Roger saw a little group of people, standing up and fighting. Other detectives were converging on the spot from which the shot had been fired.

A youth was in the middle of the surging group. Roger saw his fists wave about, saw him seized, saw fists battering at his face, saw one man with his hands round the youth's neck. On the faces of most of the men near was something so ugly that it was frightening in itself—as if they lusted for blood.

Yard men had reached the group, and were struggling to get to the youth.

Other people were standing, getting in Roger's way. He elbowed his way past, rapping words out:

"Police—let us through! Police—let us through!"

He drew nearer.

Other Yard men nearer to the youth had been thrust to one side. The youth looked limp, now, his face deathly pale, as fists smashed into him; one pair of hands was still clenched viciously round his throat.

Men were shouting:

"String him up!"

"Break his neck!"

"Tear him to pieces."

Sloan tried to whisper in Roger's ear.

"If we show our guns—"

"It'll drive 'em mad," Roger growled. He roared, "Police, police! Let him go!"

He had to smash his way through the crowd now, but some men kept their heads, several were pulling the vicious ones off the youth, who seemed to have fainted. As he fell, the man trying to strangle him was prized away.

Women were watching, terrified; a few fainted.

In the tension of the moment, it was easy to forget the rest of the crowd. Roger knew there was a bright light, but did not know that one of the spotlights had been turned toward them.

He reached the youth, and hauled him up. Other Yard men and some of the audience were ready to help, now.

"Get the gun," Roger ordered. "Then gangway, please. Bill—" he barked to Sloan. "Take his feet."

He had the youth's shoulders.

He wasn't sure whether the youth was alive or dead. In a few seconds the face had been smashed almost beyond recognition; the bruises were swelling rapidly.

"Gangway, please!"

The cry was taken up.

There was another sound—a voice over the loud-speaker. Matthewson began to talk quite calmly.

"Ladies and gentlemen, it will help if everyone will remain seated, just for a few minutes. That will also help the police—after all, that's why we're here, isn't it—to help the police? Sir Neville is *not* seriously injured...."

That assurance broke through the tension, forced the thoughts of the crowd away from the shooting and the prisoner back to the platform. There was a cheer, ragged at first, soon much stronger.

"A doctor is already attending him," Matthewson went on, "but as an old soldier, I know enough about gunshot wounds to be sure that this one is a glancing one which will do little serious harm."

Whether that was true or false, it calmed the crowd.

150

Roger and Sloan were at one of the circular corridors at the back of the hall. Other police took the
youth from them. The gun was a .32 automatic;
Roger now had it.

"Get a doctor for him," Roger said. "See that he's
kept away from the crowd."

"Yes, sir."

"Bill, we want one or two of those fellows who
started to tear him to bits," Roger said. "Hurry."

Chatworth, just behind them, heard that.

"Why?"

"Mustn't let 'em get away with it," Roger said,
and pushed past the A.C. "That way we'll ask for
mob law." He was already hurrying back to the
spot. "There was a fellow in blue, with a red bow
tie," he said to Sloan. "Another chap with a scar on
his right cheek. They'll do." He stood at the end of
the rows looking for the pair. "There they are."

Other police had followed.

Roger called, "You, sir—" He pointed. "And
you—" He pointed again. Men looked at him. "Just
a moment, please, we'd like a word with you."

They came without argument. It wasn't until he
got them in the gangways that he charged them
with assault. They looked shocked. The man who
had nearly strangled—perhaps had strangled—
the life out of the youth, was astounded. Now that
passion was spent, he was just an ordinary, mild-
mannered man.

As they walked along the passage, Matthewson
was saying:

" ...And so the Citizens' League proposes to form
its own force, of vigilantes, public-spirited men
and women—yes, and women—who will band together to protect their lives and property, until the

151

police forces are strong enough and sufficiently armed ..."

Roger, Sloan and the two prisoners went out of earshot. Chatworth was nowhere in sight. Roger handed the two men over to uniformed police, who took them downstairs and had them sent to the Yard.

The youthful gunman was still unconscious.

Roger and Sloan went to the rooms beneath the platform. A few policemen and some of the organizers were standing about. Chatworth was among them, with several pressmen. Brammer was among these, looking sardonic as Roger appeared.

"Have you got the gunman, Handsome?"

"Yes."

"Name—"

"Later," Roger said. "If you and the rest of the newspapermen have any sense, you'll run a story on the folly of individuals taking the law into their own hands. They nearly choked the life out of him."

"But, Handsome," Brammer protested mildly, "that's the mood they're in. Didn't you notice?"

"How's Hann-Gorlay?" Roger asked abruptly.

"He'll be all right," said Brammer.

Roger and Sloan went into a dressing room where the injured M.P. was lying. Ruth was there, a doctor, several other people. Ruth saw Roger, but didn't move toward him. Hann-Gorlay was lying on his back, and the doctor was putting adhesive plaster on his temple. The injured man was conscious, and there was some color in his cheeks.

Chatworth came in as Roger moved toward Hann-Gorlay.

"Remember me?" he asked. "I'm Chief Inspector West of New Scotland Yard." He didn't give Hann-Gorlay time to respond. "If you've any sense at all, you'll stop this campaign before you do a hell of a lot more damage than the young brutes themselves are doing. If it had got any worse outside, there would have been a panic in that hall, with hundreds injured, perhaps dozens crushed to death. You'd have been as responsible for that as anyone else. Widows, orphans and idiots wouldn't stop to think you did it for what you thought was best. That wouldn't make any difference to them —they'd still be widows, orphans and idiots." His voice was harsh, angry. "For God's sake, drop this idiocy before it goes too far."

He stopped.

Ruth Linder pushed her way forward, until she was by Hann-Gorlay's side.

"I think that's more than enough, Chief Inspector."

"Don't stop him, Ruth," said Hann-Gorlay. His voice was smooth, he had recovered almost completely, showed no sign of strain or shock. "We have to expect opposition even from the police themselves, of course—especially from senior officers. The fewer there are of them, the greater the glory they share." The words were meant as an insult.

"Listen to me," Roger said. "You've weakened the police force more tonight than twenty bandit holdups would have done. That's only a beginning. If you get an armed corps of vigilantes, then every young fool who wants to break into a house will know he's likely to face an armed man and—"

"He'll think again!"

"He'll take a gun."

"They take guns already."

"Look," said Roger, almost desperately, "you want a *little* sense of proportion. We had three hundred and forty-one burglaries or robberies in the Great London area last week. In fourteen cases the crooks were armed. That's one in twenty. You're going to turn it into one in every two or three. Then we'll have a job so big we'll never be able to tackle it. Can't you—"

"Very persuasive," sneered Hann-Gorlay. "Darling, I think I'm well enough to go back to the meetings. They do expect me, don't they?"

Roger shot a glance at Chatworth.

"We could hold him—on grounds of causing a breach of peace."

Chatworth said, "Let the fool go."

"Darling—" Hann-Gorlay took Ruth's arm as he stood up by the side of the couch. He looked a little less pale. "Will you lead the way?"

"Are you sure you're fit?" Ruth began.

"Of course I'm sure; I'm perfectly all right."

They moved toward the door.

Roger blocked their path.

"Wait a minute," he said. They stopped. "You'll get a big cheer when you show your face there again. You know that. You had them where you wanted them before, now you'll be able to do what you like with them. But you might regret it. The murderers might have planned this carefully. They might have a second gunman waiting to finish the job the first one started."

"Be good enough to move aside," Hann-Gorlay said stiffly.

The youthful prisoner was still unconscious. Letters in his pockets showed that he was Edgar Randall, with an address in Fulham. Detectives were soon on the way to the address.

"Have him taken to a nursing home," Roger said. "And keep me in touch." He poked his fingers through his hair, and glanced at Sloan; Chatworth hadn't left the room below the platform. "Let's go and hear what Hann-Gorlay's saying now, Bill. He's got guts, but I'd like—" He didn't finish.

The great hall was hushed, but for Hann-Gorlay's voice. He was speaking very quietly. The spotlight made him look like an Adonis—and the patch of plaster over his right temple must have caught the imagination of the crowd.

"...It is now evident that these vicious youths, these depraved brutes, will stop at nothing. Knowing the police are not armed, they will take the risk, the almost negligible risk, of coming here and of attempting to prevent the people from organizing themselves. But I know the people *better* than they—"

He won the deep-throated roar of applause that he obviously wanted.

"...and our Citizens' League must organize itself, must patrol the streets of our home towns and our suburbs. Its members must band themselves together, become so strong that they will stop these brutes from daring to attack. For this—you will all understand so well—for this we need money. We cannot forever be maintained by one or two newspapers. So we have arranged for stewards to go among you. We know that you will give everything you can spare toward this cause, this very great cause..."

Roger watched and listened, hands thrust deep in his pockets, cigarette jutting out from his lips. Sloan was fidgety. After a few seconds, Hann-Gorlay sat down. Ruth leaned across to speak to him. Matthewson got up, to set the collection in motion. The whole crowd was in movement, men taking out their wallets, women their purses. Stewards with collecting bags and plates were busy.

"We aren't going to have any more trouble to-night," Sloan said. "Not here, anyhow. I wonder what's been happening outside."

Roger shrugged.

"Let's get back to the Yard. Chatworth came in his own car, we needn't worry about him."

Outside in the crisp night air great crowds had gathered; the police were still having difficulty in keeping them from trying to force their way into the Hall. Men were standing on soapboxes and in doorways, holding impromptu meetings, all with the same theme as Hann-Gorlay's.

Roger switched on the radio, and got through to the Yard.

"West here. Is there anything—"

"We're having a *hell* of a night," he was told. "Trouble in nearly every Division. We just haven't the men to go round."

17

Bad Night

It was one o'clock in the morning.

Chatworth sat in the small armchair in front of the fireplace in Roger's office. Sloan and Peel were present. Peel put some small coal on a dying fire, and made it completely black.

Chatworth took a half-smoked cigar from his lips, and looked at it.

"How many burglaries?" he asked Roger.

"Seventeen, sir—that's not exceptional for a dark night. But nine were with violence. Two policemen were shot, another was coshed, a third slashed with a razor. Out of the raiders we picked up one man in HK Division. He fell from a roof, and is unconscious—they're going to advise me as soon as he comes round." Roger stood up. "It's time I went to Ruth Linder's flat in Wilmington Place, I think. And you, Bill."

Chatworth looked rather like a sulky bulldog.

"Why?"

"Hann-Gorlay and Ruth Linder are still at a night club they went to after the Albert Hall show. They like the gay life after their serious work, don't

157

they? I think there's a risk that they'll be shot at as they turn up at her flat. In any case, I want to talk to her again." Roger seemed to be defying Chatworth to tell him not to go; but Chatworth simply jabbed his cigar back between his lips. "I've arranged for Matthewson and the other organizers of the Citizens' League to be watched—they're sticking their necks out."

"Hmmm," grunted Chatworth. "You ought to know, you've been doing it for long enough. Do you know *anything* more than you did a month ago?" He wasn't being nasty.

"Not much."

"Can you think of any good reason why anyone should want to make the police vicious?" Chatworth asked, as if that were the one thing he couldn't understand. "If there were any sense in it at all—" He broke off.

Roger said, "I wonder if it's too easy to assume that this is all one organized campaign? The *Courier*, and that means Brammer, started the idea. Nearly everyone else has jumped to the same conclusion. I get less and less sure that they're right. There's one organized gang, I should say, but a lot of these youths are on their own. It's much too big to be one group of people under a central direction. There are a few indications that Prescott was connected with some other killer, and we know he had guns for another seven. We haven't proved that he ever worked with anyone else, though."

Roger lit a cigarette, and the telephone rang while he was doing so.

Peel answered, and they all waited.

Peel said, "Okay," and rang off. "They've called

for their bill at the night club, Roger, and should be at her flat in twenty minutes or so."

"Shall we talk about this again tomorrow?" Roger asked Chatworth.

Chatworth said, "No, finish it now; I'll come downstairs with you." Three of them hurried out, leaving Peel in solitary possession of the office. "Go on, Roger."

"I've been checking all the stolen stuff we found at Prescott's place. It comes from two robberies only. We've picked up other odds and ends of stuff which we know some of these violent robbers took. There are indications that all the rest was sold through various channels." They were at the lift, and Sloan pressed the bell push for it. "In other words, the crimes appear to be isolated, not organized—different fences are used, the kind of crime is varied. Looked at as a whole, I'd say that it isn't *all* of a piece. There's probably a small group, or gang, setting examples, but not every young swine with a gun or a cosh is in it. There's nothing I'd like better than to hang it all round one person's neck, but I can't. It's much too big. Young desperadoes have simply become infected."

The lift arrived; they stepped in.

"A small gang, setting an example?" Chatworth echoed. "Inspirational, so to speak."

"That's it, sir. The man Harrock, who killed Uncle Benny, had done one or two jobs with violence—we know that now." Roger was earnest. "Prescott on his own did a good job on that Putney bank. There weren't any signs that he had anyone else with him. Most of the other jobs are the same —individual jobs. It's true that Prescott had ni-

159

troglycerine with him, and that most of them use .32 guns, but—"

They jolted to a standstill, stepped out.

"What's on your mind?" Chatworth demanded.

"It just hadn't got the smack of organized gang warfare with a central headquarters. I've been over this until I know it backward," Roger went on as they hurried down the steps toward his car. "If it weren't for the .32's and the newspaper campaign story, no one would have thought about an organized gang or a campaign until those threatening notes were posted. The crimes came first; then someone who hates our guts cashed in, began to work up the temperature. It could be a group of youths with more imagination than most. It could be—" He broke off.

Chatworth said, "Well, don't overdo it. Or you, Sloan. We haven't got our strength doubled yet. Still got that gun, Roger?"

"Yes, sir."

"Keep it. Good night."

"Good night, sir," they said in chorus.

Roger swung the car out of the Yard, onto the Embankment, and then toward Parliament Square. The night was very dark. There was no car or taxi, no traffic at all, in all the wide, spacious breadth of Whitehall; London might have been a ghost city.

There were a few taxis and private cars near Piccadilly Circus—one or two cyclists, too, but the road leading to Wilmington Place was deserted. Roger pulled up at the end of the street, and they got out. The shadowy figure of a waiting policeman came toward him.

"Are we late?" Roger asked.

"They're not back yet," the man said.

"Any trouble?"

"Nothing at all."

"Good," said Roger.

He got out of the car, and Sloan followed him. The two watching detectives moved back into the darkness. There was no sound for fully ten minutes. Then a car engine sounded, and headlights showed. The light grew brighter, soon the car swung round the corner.

Standing in a doorway, Roger and Sloan weren't touched by the white brilliance.

The car turned in at the drive of Wilmington Court. It stopped abruptly—too abruptly. The headlights were switched off, but nothing else happened. A porter appeared from the main entrance of the block of flats, and quickly backed away again.

"What is this?" Sloan growled.

"Necking, probably," Roger said. "Let's go and see what mood they're in."

He led the way. No one in the doorway or in the car appeared to notice them. Only the car's sidelights were on. As he drew nearer, Roger could just make out the shape of the two people in the car—man and woman, their heads very close together. Nearer still, and he could see that they were kissing. Their faces showed up against the light of the block of flats.

Roger passed the front of the car; so did Sloan, but they weren't noticed.

Sloan was grinning when they reached the doorway.

"I wonder how long they'll keep this up."

161

He glanced about him, and nodded to the night porter, who approached slowly, perhaps nervously.

"It's all right," Roger said. "Police, I want to see Miss Linder."

"She's just arrived, sir."

"So I noticed!"

Roger lit a cigarette. The luxurious entrance hall was pleasantly warm. He strolled again to an arm-chair and sat down; Sloan stayed near the entrance, watching the car, although he could hardly make out the shape of the two people in it.

With the policeman on duty outside, and Sloan watching, surely nothing could go wrong. Roger found himself wondering whether there had ever been any real justification for thinking that Ruth and Hann-Gorlay would be shot at when they reached here.

The chair was comfortable. For a reason he couldn't fully understand, Roger felt more relaxed than he had for some time. He found himself thinking of Janet. Then he began to wonder if the kissing and the cuddling in the car suggested that wedding bells were in the offing. Ruth wouldn't be likely to sell herself cheap, and to a man like Hann-Gorlay the price would probably be marriage.

"They're breaking the clinch." Sloan grinned across.

The car door opened and slammed. The porter hurried out. There were voices—Hann-Gorlay's loudest. He came in with his arm round Ruth's waist, with the porter a discreet distance behind them. Their faces were very close together, and Ruth was flushed, her glossy black hair was untidy; she looked young, beautiful and starry-eyed.

Had it been anyone else, anyone he met casually, Roger would have felt quite sure that these two were helplessly infatuated—in the stage of obsession with each other and with love.

The porter slipped past them, and opened the lift doors.

"Darling," Ruth said, "don't come up. You've so much to do in the morning."

"Of course I'll come up," said Hann-Gorlay.

They passed Roger and Sloan, without glancing toward them. Roger was by Sloan's side, and whispered:

"We'll wait. Let 'em get upstairs—unless they spot us first."

"Okay."

Hann-Gorlay and Ruth stepped into the lift, the porter followed and closed the door.

One of the watching detectives appeared.

"All quiet out here, sir."

"Good," said Roger. "Let's try the stairs, Bill."

They went briskly up the stairs, and reached the landing as the lift started to go down again. Just a few yards along the passage, Hann-Gorlay and Ruth were in each other's arms.

Sloan whispered:

"Let's get out of here."

He was still grinning, but looked a little sheepish. Roger knew what he felt like—as if he were both eavesdropper and Peeping Tom at the same time.

The couple moved on slowly.

"Give me your key," Hann-Gorlay said.

"All right, darling. But you're not coming in tonight. In the first place, I don't trust you"—she paused, and they laughed together, as if that were the greatest joke in the world—"and in the second place, you *must* be up early. I shall be busy, too."

She handed him her key.

"I'll be good, and go home," Hann-Gorlay promised. "Oh, my darling, it's so good to be with you. Whenever I'm anywhere else it just seems like a waste of time."

He opened the door, and thrust it open.

"Good night, my sweet."

They kissed again, then Hann-Gorlay put a hand inside the door, to switch on the light.

A shot cut across the quiet so viciously that it was like a flash of lightning in a pitch-black night. It petrified all four of them—until a second shot came, and Hann-Gorlay began to crumple up.

18

Capture

Between the first and the second shots, Roger moved. Sloan was only a split second behind him.

Hann-Gorlay was on the floor, Ruth on her knees by his side, shocked, her mouth open, when Roger pushed past her and into the flat. It was in darkness.

"Careful, Roger!" Sloan roared.

Roger saw a light in a room beyond and a man against it. The door slammed, shutting the light out. He rushed toward the door, calling:

"Put on the light, Bill!"

The light came on.

Roger turned the handle of the door, and thrust his shoulder against the panels, but it was locked. He could hear sounds inside the room. He drew back, then launched himself against the door; it didn't budge.

"Both together," Sloan said, "and—"

"Wait a minute! Go downstairs, tell our chaps to watch the windows. What street side is this?"

Sloan moved toward the door.

"The porter will know."

"Hurry, and don't forget his gun."

Sloan didn't speak.

Ruth, on her knees beside Hann-Gorlay, was speaking, but Roger didn't catch the words, didn't know whether she was talking to the injured man, herself or to him. He backed away, watching the closed door. The gunman might plan to get out through the window, or might burst the door open as he tried to force his way out.

Roger heard the girl vaguely. He could shoot the lock off the door and get in; but he wanted to give Sloan time to get downstairs and have the street watched.

Sloan would soon be back.

"Neville, speak to me, speak to me." So Ruth was talking to Hann-Gorlay. There was anguish in her voice. *"Neville, you mustn't die, you mustn't die."*

With half of his mind, Roger realized what she was really saying—that Hann-Gorlay was unconscious, and looked badly injured. He ought to see what he could do; but had to watch that door.

"Oh, to let this happen to you," Ruth said piteously, *"to let it happen to you."*

Roger glanced at her sharply.

That might mean a lot more than it appeared to—seemed to imply that she could have stopped it.

She was holding a cloth, a scarf, against Hann-Gorlay's neck; and there was blood on her hand.

If Roger hadn't glanced toward her, he wouldn't have seen the foot.

Someone else was in the passage, close to the door. Ruth could only see her lover, had no time or thought for anyone else; but the polished toe of a black shoe was there.

166

Roger pressed against the wall.

He heard the sound from the room behind the locked door; there was no sound anywhere but Ruth's voice, sunk to a whisper now; Roger couldn't understand what she was saying. He drew out his gun.

The man approaching drew nearer; the barrel of an automatic showed, then the tip of the man's nose, a hand, the other foot.

The man's face appeared, and he looked round the open door—and his gun hand came into full sight. Roger fired at it. The bullet struck the wrist, bringing a sudden, agonized screech. The gun dropped.

Roger leaped, as Ruth turned her head abruptly.

The gunman backed swiftly against the wall. He was young, dark-haired, well dressed. He was Charles Mortimer.

Roger said, "Come in here, Mortimer."

He covered the man with his gun, but still had to be wary, in case the second man came out of the room. The only sound was of labored breathing. Ruth still held a handkerchief padded against Hann-Gorlay's neck, while she stared at Mortimer.

Roger had time only for a glimpse of her—yet the impression of livid hatred for the youth went very deep.

Then he heard footsteps, and Sloan's voice.

"Okay, Roger, we've got—"

Sloan stopped. He must have turned the corner, and seen the prisoner. Mortimer glanced toward him, licked his lips, then moved, crouching, as if he still hoped to get away.

"Keep still," Roger ordered. "Okay, Bill. Come and pick his gun up."

Sloan appeared, and obeyed. Mortimer crouched against the wall, watching Roger's gun. For the first time, Roger realized that the gun had really captured Mortimer; had perhaps saved his, Roger's, life. He'd used it without thinking.

This wasn't the time to think about that.

"Do you say you've caught the other chap?" he asked Sloan.

"He was shinning down the drainpipe, and jumped right into our arms," Sloan said. "Not exactly a wasted evening. You all right?"

"Yes. Make sure that Mortimer hasn't another gun."

Roger waited until Sloan ran over Mortimer's pockets. The youth was holding his right arm up, clasping the wounded wrist to stop the bleeding. Months ago, Prescott had done some thing like that after being injured at the bank.

"You take him downstairs," Roger said. "I'll phone for a doctor. Patrol cars here yet?"

"One is."

"Good."

Roger went to Ruth. She was still on her knees, still holding the pad, but it had slipped a little. Hann-Gorlay had been shot just beneath the chin. It was an ugly wound, the kind which might kill quickly. The man looked pale as death; might be dead already.

"Miss Linder!" Roger barked.

She looked round at him, startled.

"I'll take over from you. Telephone for a doctor." He actually had to take her arms and pull her up. Then he dropped down onto one knee, folding a handkerchief into a pad to press against the wound, which started oozing blood again. "Hurry!" he snapped at Ruth.

She moved.

He was startled that she went so quickly—and Sloan was taken off his guard.

She simply flung herself at Charles Mortimer.

Her clenched fists beat against the youth's face and breast. He backed away desperately, trying to fend her off with his free hand. Blood from the wound in his wrist spattered her dress, even spotted her face.

Sloan dragged her off.

She looked as if rage had turned her cheeks to white heat; and her eyes burned.

"You fix the doctor, Bill," Roger said.

Ruth Linder didn't try to attack Mortimer again. She let Sloan put her into a chair, and stayed there. Then Sloan took Mortimer's arm, and started to hustle him toward the stairs and the head of the lift. Before he had gone far, men arrived from below—police from a second patrol car. There were plenty of men for everything that had to be done.

Roger stayed with Hann-Gorlay, staunching the flow of blood until a doctor arrived.

At this time Ruth Linder sat in the chair, staring straight ahead of her. She did not seem to know what she was looking at. Her eyes still burned, and her cheeks had that same glow, almost of white heat.

Hann-Gorlay was already being taken downstairs on a stretcher, and an ambulance was waiting. Charles Mortimer was in the hall with the other prisoner, a youth whose name was Gedd. Both were handcuffed.

Sloan was back upstairs with Roger.

Roger had forced open the locked door, they had complete freedom of the flat. It had been ransacked. Drawers were turned upside down and their contents scattered, pictures had been pushed to one side, cushions and upholstery ripped open. Cut glass from the dressing table was smashed. The place hadn't just been burgled—it looked as if someone who hated Ruth had come in here to smash everything to pieces.

"I'd rather act on your guess than my reason," Sloan said, as he checked the damage. "I wonder what she'll think of it."

"She doesn't seem capable of thinking about anything or anyone but Hann-Gorlay," Roger said slowly.

He went into the entrance hall of the flat.

The girl still sat there.

He crossed to her and looked down. She moved her head for the first time since Sloan had pushed her into the chair. Something of the fire had faded from her eyes—they were smoldering, but at least as much with pain as with rage. She looked as if she could burst into bitter tears.

"Is he—dead?"

"No," Roger said, brusquely. "From what the police surgeon said, he'll probably pull through."

"Are you—" she caught her breath. "Are you *sure?*"

"There's a good chance."

"Where is he? I must go to him. Where—" She jumped up, shrill, eager.

"Take it easy," Roger said, and took her arm. "I

should sit down again, Ruth. Bill, get her a drink, will you? And then have one of the boys put on a kettle and make her some tea. Hann-Gorlay's on his way to hospital, Ruth; you won't be able to see him tonight. I'll keep you informed about his condition." He was still brusque, but with a sort of rough kindliness. "I have to know what's missing from the flat."

In fact, he wanted to give her something to do.

"As if that matters," she said.

"It matters a lot."

She shrugged.

Sloan brought her a whisky and soda, and she sipped it. One of the patrolmen made tea. Roger was anxious to talk to Mortimer and Gedd, but didn't want to leave the girl for long. He left Sloan to talk to her and make a note of what she said, then hurried downstairs.

The police surgeon had patched up Mortimer's wrist; no one had done anything about the scratches on his cheeks, caused by Ruth's nails. His arm was in a homemade sling, and as Roger went toward him, the police surgeon said:

"Better get him to hospital, Handsome."

"All right, soon," Roger said. "Mortimer, why did you burgle Miss Linder's place?"

Mortimer didn't answer.

"Keeping quiet won't help you," Roger said. "You're in bad trouble. You took part in an armed burglary, and as you carried a gun, you'll get almost as much punishment as if you'd fired the shots yourself. If Hann-Gorlay dies, you'll be up on a hanging charge, as accessory. The only way to ease things for yourself is to talk."

Mortimer looked defiant. The scratches and

weals showed up clearly on his cheek, the only streaks of color against his pallor.

"Why burgle Ruth Linder's place?" Roger repeated. "She's a friend of yours, isn't she? She's sold you jewelry at bargain prices. Why turn against her?"

Mortimer didn't speak.

"Handsome, we don't want trouble with that wrist," the police surgeon said. "You know what will happen if he complains that he wasn't looked after properly."

"I'd look after him," Roger growled. "Where will you take him?"

"St. Thomas's. Where Hann-Gorlay's gone."

"I shouldn't think they'll have to keep Mortimer in," Roger said. "As soon as possible, we'll have him at the Yard."

He detailed two men to go with Mortimer.

Gedd, who had actually shot Hann-Gorlay, was a different type. He couldn't be more than nineteen or twenty. He was plump and curly-haired and rosy-cheeked. His blue eyes were bright and falsely candid, and he didn't seem even mildly resentful or remorseful.

He was smoking a cigarette, and standing nonchalantly against the wall, handcuffed to a hefty plain-clothes man. He listened to the talk between Roger and the police surgeon with a half grin— and the grin was still on his face when Roger turned to him.

"What's funny?" Roger demanded. "The thought of hanging?"

Gedd said, "Who cares?"

Roger said softly, "God knows why she should,

but your mother, for one. Perhaps your father, too. It's bad luck when they get swine like you for a child, but they feel just as deeply about it."

Gedd sneered.

"That gooey crap—forget it."

"So you're tough."

"They don't grow any tougher."

"Why did you burgle Miss Linder's flat?"

"Doesn't she wear jools?"

"Do you know her?"

"If I know her, what about it?"

"Do you?"

"She can dance," Gedd sneered. "She can afford to lose some of her sparklers, too. This'll teach her to go around with that lap dog with a title."

"Were you waiting there to shoot him?"

"Why don't you stop asking me questions?" Gedd demanded, and yawned. It wasn't a natural yawn, it was meant to be insulting. "You make me tired."

"I'll do something else with you before I've finished," Roger said, and looked up at a C.I.D. man. "Take him to the Yard. Don't give him an armchair or any more cigarettes."

Gedd drew smoke from the cigarette in his mouth, and blew it into Roger's face. Roger clenched his fists as he spun round. Gedd laughed, jeeringly. The detective jerked him away and took him out; another detective joined them as they reached the door.

A uniformed policeman on duty said, "There's a lot of them like that these days, sir—can't do anything with them. Callous beasts, that's what they are—they kill for the sake of killing. I've never

173

known anything like it in my twenty-six years with the Force."

"I can believe it," Roger growled.

He walked upstairs, wanting to take his time. The attitude of the prisoner and the remark of the constable seemed to start a new train of thought. But was it so new? Hadn't he been talking about it with Chatworth? There was an ugly, dangerous spirit abroad. Too many youths like Gedd took exactly the same defiant attitude. That was one explanation of the present crime wave. It wasn't just a matter of organized gangs; there was a callous, murderous spirit in the air.

What had happened to young Mortimer? Why had he turned on Ruth?

Roger turned into the passage leading to Ruth's flat.

He saw men photographing the blood on the carpet—blood from Hann-Gorlay's throat wound. He remembered the way Ruth had knelt over him, her moaning words, her vicious attack. The words mattered.

"Oh, to let this happen to you."

He would tackle her about that now.

He turned into the entrance hall.

Sloan came hurrying—and Sloan had news that really counted. His voice was tense with excitement.

"Come and see what we've found." He was as pleased as Peel had been with the red Morris as he led the way into the drawing room. It was still in a state of hopeless confusion—in fact, was worse than before, because the corners of the carpet were rolled up and some floor boards had been raised.

174

Jewels were spread about on the floor in one corner.

"All stolen stuff," Sloan said. "We've caught her with the goods, Roger."

19

Arrest

Roger picked up several of the pieces of jewelry. He recognized two as having been stolen in recent raids—in one, a policeman had been wounded.

"That's probably what the brutes came for," Sloan said. "They knew she had the stuff, and thought that it would be an easy picking."

"Could be." Roger was tense. "Where is she?"

"In her bedroom."

"Alone?"

"Yes."

"We mustn't leave her alone," Roger said, sharply. "Don't take any chance with her." He strode toward the door of the bedroom. "After the way she flew at Mortimer, I'd back her to do anything crazy, such as cut her own throat."

The door wasn't locked; yet Roger had half expected Ruth to lock herself in. She was sitting by the dressing table, still dressed for out of doors, with a mink wrap round her shoulders, looking at her reflection in a gilt-framed mirror. The chaotic state of the bedroom didn't seem to worry her at all. Her face was blank. All the life, that deep, powerful vitality, had gone. She was a ghost of herself.

She glanced round, but didn't show any sign that she recognized them.

Roger went toward her, then pulled up a chair. Sloan stood watching and listening. Roger proffered cigarettes, and she refused.

"Mind if I smoke?"

"Do as you wish."

"Thanks." He lit up. "You knew Mortimer, of course—how well did you know Gedd?"

"Gedd? Was he—"

"*He* shot Hann-Gorlay."

There was a spark of interest, of anger, in her eyes.

"I thought Mortimer—"

"He was just on guard."

"Gedd is"—she caught her breath—"a little swine."

"Yes. How long have you known him?"

"Three or four months."

"How did you come to meet him?"

"Mortimer brought him along to a party."

"Just to a party?"

"That's right."

"Why should they burgle this flat?"

"They knew there would be something worth taking here, I suppose," she said. "Must I answer—"

"Yes. Do you know of any special reason?"

"No."

"What is the relationship between you and all of these young men, Miss Linder?"

"They're friends of mine. I have *girl* friends as well. They're just—" She shrugged, and the spark

177

went out. "They're just friends of mine. I can't help it if some of them are—" She didn't finish.

"Criminals?"

She didn't answer.

"Are you sure you don't know what they came here for?" Roger insisted.

"I've told you what I think."

"I'll tell you what I *know*," Roger said. "Come with me, please."

Until then she hadn't really been interested. Now she was—and she looked puzzled. Roger reminded himself that she might be an expert at fooling him.

She got up and followed, and Sloan brought up the rear.

Several more pieces of jewelry had been found under the floor boards, and the plain-clothes man there was on his knees.

He picked up a diamond pendant.

"That's from the Ling Hotel job in Kensington, sir—no doubt about that."

"Thanks," said Roger, and looked at Ruth.

She stood quite still.

For the first time since Hann-Gorlay had been taken away, she seemed to be shaken out of herself. She held herself rigid. Her eyes were rounded, and she stared at the jewelry as if at fearful things.

She darted a quick glance at Roger.

"Is that what they came for?" Roger demanded.

"I—" she began in a cracked voice, and then stopped.

"Is it?"

"I didn't—I didn't know that was there." She gulped as she finished. Her expression told him

178

plainly that she knew that she wasn't likely to be believed. "I just didn't know—"

She broke off. The glow in her eyes was almost one of appeal; in that moment Roger could believe that she was begging him to believe her story.

The glow faded, and she moved toward a chair. As she dropped into it, she was trembling.

"Very convincing," Roger sneered. "There's a small fortune in stolen stuff there, Ruth—all stolen by young brutes like Mortimer and Gedd. Stolen by killers. I always warned you what would happen if you went on with your uncle's game."

She stayed mute.

Roger said, "You've had a hell of a shock tonight. I don't want to make things worse for you than they are." He made himself speak more quietly. "Can you give any explanation about these jewels?"

She didn't answer.

"Can you?"

She opened her eyes. They had changed again. She had looked just like this when he had seen her at the shop in the Mile End Road; when she had shown the depths of her bitterness toward and her hatred of the police.

"I did not know they were there," she said, carefully.

Roger said, "That doesn't help." He became very formal. "You know I've no alternative but to charge you, Miss Linder, don't you?"

She said nothing.

"It's my duty to charge you with being in the possession of certain items of jewelry, knowing them to be stolen," Roger went on, "and I have to

179

warn you that anything you say may be used in evidence."

She said slowly, vehemently, "I always knew the police would frame me, sooner or later."

They were taking her along the passage when the lift gates opened, and Brammer and Pauline Weston came out.

Brammer raised one hand, as if astounded—and then stared at Ruth. He didn't smile and he didn't gloat. Pauline closed her eyes. There wasn't any doubt that she knew Ruth. Seeing her, Roger's thoughts flashed back to the fact that her car might have been used in his kidnaping; that Mortimer was a friend of hers, she was well in with these youths—who might be members of a big gang.

Might be? Couldn't he be sure, now?

Ruth said, "And Brammer helped to frame me, West. He's responsible for all this. Even if you put me in jail the trouble will go on. He—"

"So they've caught you," Brammer said heavily.

"Bram—" began Pauline Weston. She was close to him, and took his hand. She wore a black suit and a fur cape and a silly little black hat. She looked about nineteen—an innocent nineteen. "Come away."

"It's all right, my sweet, I'm not going to tell her how glad I am," Brammer said. "Any use asking the charge, Handsome?"

"You can find out later, at the Yard," Roger said stiffly.

They went into the lift, with Ruth between them. Pauline Weston stood just by Brammer's side, on the landing. She gave Roger a queer impression that she would like to help, that she understood something of what Ruth Linder felt.

The lift carried them below the landing; Brammer's and Pauline's legs and feet disappeared. Pauline had lovely legs.

Ruth Linder didn't speak on her way to Cannon Row, where she was to be held for the night. Once they were inside the gray, forbidding-looking police station which was beneath the shadow of the Yard she broke the silence. She seemed to do so with an effort—as if there were just one thing stronger than her hatred of the police.

"Will you find out how Nev—how Hann-Gorlay is?"

"Yes," Roger promised.

A woman police officer took Ruth into a room for searching. Roger went along to the duty sergeant's desk, put a call in to the hospital where Hann-Gorlay had been taken, and talked to the sergeant while waiting for the call to come through.

Then: "This is Scotland Yard—inquiring after Sir Neville Hann-Gorlay, please."

"Just one moment, sir; I'll put you through to the house surgeon."

Roger waited another two or three minutes before the doctor came on the line. He was brief. Hann-Gorlay was unconscious, and likely to be for some time. The bullet hadn't struck any vital part, and had missed the carotid artery by half an inch. It would be surprising if he didn't pull through.

"Good," said Roger briskly. "Thanks."

He gave Ruth the report as soon as she had been searched and was ready for a cell—quite well furnished, just an ordinary room with bars in place of one wall. The girl's eyes brightened for a moment, and the bitterness, the hatred was dimmed.

"Thank you," she said stiffly.

Then she turned away.

Gedd and Mortimer wouldn't say anything more. Roger made a hurried visit to their flat— Gedd now shared Mortimer's—in Bayswater. A few oddments of stolen goods were found, this time, and a .32 automatic as well as thirty-one rounds of ammunition. It would be morning before their recent movements and their friends' could be traced.

Tomorrow would be a hell of a day.

Roger reached home soon after four o'clock, didn't disturb Janet—and wasn't disturbed by Janet or the boys when they got up. He woke just after ten. He was alone in the room, and could hear someone singing out in the street; the singing stopped. A vacuum began to drone somewhere downstairs. He smiled faintly.

It wasn't long before Janet put her head round the door.

"What's the pandemonium about?" demanded Roger. "Must we spring-clean on the only hour I have in bed?"

She made a *moue* at him, moved across, and kissed him lightly on the forehead, then straightened up. He wouldn't let her go, but pulled her down.

There were a few brief, precious moments, before she jerked herself free.

"How's the Public Hero—thirsty?"

"Not to say hungry. Who made me a hero?"

"Brammer—and most of the newspapers. They say that you stopped panic at the Albert Hall by having so many men on duty there. There's nothing but the Albert Hall shooting and the—the robberies on the front page. *And* your photograph."

"Buttering by Brammer," murmured Roger. "They haven't run the story of Ruth Linder's arrest yet, I suppose?"

Janet's eyes sparkled.

"*Have* you got her?"

Roger told her what had happened at Wilmington Place. The story of the second attack on Hann-Gorlay would be in the early editions of the evening papers—which would soon be on the London streets. Before long he would be wanted to answer questions at the Yard.

Ruth was to be charged at Great Marlborough Street at noon; he would ask for an eight-day remand. He could go straight to the police court from here, then on to the Yard.

Janet said slowly:

"You aren't exactly overjoyed, are you?"

"What about?"

"Arresting Ruth Linder."

"Aren't I?" asked Roger, and grinned again. "Green get in your eyes?"

"*Are* you?"

Roger said, "Yes and no. I can't see why she should be crazy enough to keep the stolen stuff in that flat. She's always known that we were watching her, that we believed she was up to the fencing game. So she knew that if she made the slightest slip, the flat would be searched. Which means she was deliberately asking for trouble. Would she do that?"

After a pause, Janet said:

"And what?"

Roger patted her shoulder.

"She *looked* so innocent. Love has taken the wickedness out of her! Start getting breakfast, sweetheart; I'll nip through a shave."

Before shaving, he telephoned the hospital. Hann-Gorlay had had a comfortable night, and was in no danger. He phoned the Yard, too. Nothing else had happened—except that the prisoner who had been caught early in the evening and had fallen off a roof had come round. He hadn't talked. He'd had a .32 pistol, but there was nothing at his flat to help the police.

The policeman watching Pauline Weston had nothing to report.

Roger was worried about this attitude to the girl; to the fact that she popped up so often, with Brammer. She had a foot in both camps, was a friend of proven desperadoes. She *could* be Brammer's liaison with the young crooks, if Brammer were involved.

Roger ate sausages and bubble-and-squeak, read the newspapers and spared an occasional word for Janet, who busied herself about the kitchen. When there was a knock at the front door, she went to open it. She was soon back.

"Will you see Brammer?" she asked, "or shall I tell him you're too busy?"

20

Remand

Brammer looked very tall and gaunt—and as if he hadn't had any sleep at all. He was drawing at a cigarette which dropped from the corner of his mouth, and he seemed to move his body with an effort as he stirred to get out of an armchair.

"Sit back," Roger said.

He went to the cupboard where he kept his whisky, and took out a bottle, poured a nip and handed it to the tall man.

"Teaching me bad habits?" Brammer said, and tossed it down. "Thanks."

"Why no sleep?" asked Roger. "Excited because we've held Ruth Linder?"

"She really had the stuff at her flat, didn't she?"

"We didn't plant it there."

Brammer licked his lips, as if to get the very last taste of the whisky. He took the cigarette out, and gave a twisted grin. His eyes looked very heavy; left in the chair alone for five minutes, he would probably fall asleep.

"For the first time, I'm beginning to doubt whether she's behind it."

From Brammer, that was sensational.

"Why?"

"It makes her out to be a fool," Brammer said. "She *couldn't* be fool enough to keep stolen stuff in her flat—hot stuff, at that."

Roger didn't speak.

"You must have seen that, too," said Brammer. "I don't get it. It looks as if someone's trying to frame her. You wouldn't think that I'd try anything like that, would you?"

"Wouldn't I?"

Brammer grinned.

"I wish I knew what goes on in that thing you call a mind, Handsome."

"Nothing much," Roger said. "Nothing you'd approve of. You helped to start this Citizens' League and vigilante talk. You may have good intentions, but you're taking us to hell. Is Ruth all you came to see me about?"

"No."

"What else?"

"I've a guilty conscience."

"Forget all the old stuff."

Brammer didn't look amused. In fact looked as if he didn't like what he was about to say. He lit a fresh cigarette, and took his time lighting it. Then:

"Pauline's a nice girl. Why are you following her around so much?"

Roger said easily, "Among other things, Ruth Linder named her, said that she thought that she was worth watching. She didn't explain why she thought so."

"Oh," said Brammer. His smile became a little easier. "So Ruth was smacking at me, too. You

186

must have had quite a job trying to decide who was lying. Pauline has a black Morris Minor."

"Show me a man or woman who owns a red one," Roger said. Surely Brammer knew that Pauline's had been painted.

"It was red—until the day after you were kidnaped," Brammer declared. "It's one of those things I didn't find out until I discovered that your men were watching Pauline. I thought of Pauline's red Morris, and discovered what had happened to it. We know she's a friend of Charles Mortimer, don't we? She's a chemist, too, and probably has access to morphia and a hypo."

"I'll go and have another chat with her soon." Roger picked up the receiver, but didn't dial Whitehall 1212. "Why give me all this? Don't you love her any more?"

"You may not believe it, but I want you to put all the swine in this business behind bars," Brammer said. "Everyone, without exception and without mercy." His voice and his eyes were very hard. "Let me tell you something, Handsome. I was once in love with Ruth. I thought she was sent straight from heaven for me. I didn't care a damn about her Uncle Benny. *She* was all right. Then I came to the conclusion that she wasn't. It wouldn't help you to know why—it wouldn't convince you. It did me. We forgot all about being in love.

"We broke things off a year ago.

"Now I'm just a man with two arms, two legs, two eyes—just a man. I met Pauline, and she's quite something. I met her through Charles Mortimer." He paused, then went on very slowly, "It hurt like hell when I lost Ruth. Losing Pauline would hurt more. But if she's in this, she stands with the rest."

Roger said, "When you start a crusade, you really start it, don't you?"

He rang the Yard while Brammer looked on.

Sloan was already at his office.

"I'm going straight to Great Marborough Street," Roger told him. "Then I'm going to see Pauline Weston. Have another man put on her tail, will you?"

"Right," said Sloan. "I hope the beak will remand Ruth in custody. Are you hopeful?"

"Not very," Roger said.

Brammer agreed that he ought to be in bed, but insisted on going to the police court. There had been a long list that morning, and Ruth didn't come into the dock until twenty past twelve.

Roger gave formal evidence of arrest, and asked for an eight-day remand in custody.

"On behalf of Miss Linder," said a suave-voiced man who rose up from the solicitors' benches, "I would like to apply for bail, your worship, in any reasonable recognizances. My client is quite innocent, of course, and it would be a grievous wrong if she were compelled to undergo the indignity of prison—"

"Thank you, Mr. Scott," interrupted the magistrate, and looked at Roger. "Are there any particular reasons why you want the remand to be in custody, Chief Inspector?"

"Yes, your worship. The jewelry found in the possession of the accused is part of the proceeds of certain robberies with violence. We feel that the fullest inquiries can only be made if the accused is in custody."

In the public gallery, plump, bright-eyed Sol Klein was fidgeting, and looking as if at any moment he would jump up from his seat and speak.

The magistrate looked at Ruth. She was pale-faced, and standing quite still. Probably every man in the court was affected by her beauty. She had the sense not to flaunt it, and was dressed in quiet gray.

"Your worship," said the suave-voiced solicitor smoothly, "the police are already prejudicing the circumstances. My client has never stood in dock before, she has a most reputable past, and it is not customary for the police to apply for remand in custody on such a charge as this."

That was always the trouble, Roger knew. Precedent. The magistrate probably knew that she ought to be kept in jail for the eight days—but how could he justify such a decision? There were cases where the police could make out a case that was unarguable. Here, they couldn't.

"Have you anything to say?" the magistrate asked Ruth.

"No, sir." Her voice was very low. "Except that I know nothing about these jewels."

The magistrate tapped the bench with his gavel.

"Very well! I will remand the accused for eight days against two sureties of a thousand pounds each."

He shot a glance at Roger, almost as if in apology, then looked at the suave-voiced solicitor.

"You are very good, your worship," the man said; "I will gladly find two such sureties...."

Roger wanted to give a lot more time to questioning Pauline Weston. Pressure of other, waiting jobs made it impossible. When he saw her in his office, soon after the Magistrate's Court hearing, she seemed as cool and aloof as he had ever known her. He felt sure that he wasn't getting all the truth but he couldn't ruffle her outward serenity or trick her into contradicting herself.

Why had she been so friendly with Mortimer?

He seemed a nice boy, if a bit intense.

"Didn't you know he was a rogue?"

"If I had, I wouldn't have been friendly."

"Why did you lend him your car?"

"He hadn't one of his own."

"Miss Weston, look at the *facts*. You're a young woman of good family, good taste, with many friends in your own circle. Why did you let youths like Mortimer and Gedd use your car, and behave as if it belonged to them?"

"I thought they would look after it."

"But why—"

"I'm sorry if I choose my friends badly," Pauline murmured. There was a steely strength in her; was it feline, too?

Roger switched the subject swiftly.

"Has Brammer used your car much?"

"Bram can hardly fold himself up and get inside!"

At the end of the interview, Roger was sure that she hadn't explained her real reason for being friendly with Mortimer. But he had so much other, pressing work to do that he had to give up trying with her for the time being.

She went off, walking with that matchless grace along the Yard's bleak corridors.

Roger put her out of his mind, hammering away at Mortimer and Gedd without making them crack. There was Brammer to cover, and Matthewson and the League; Chatworth and a restless Home Office; the strident newspapers. There were routine reports to study by the hundred, more burglaries with violence, and that atmosphere of fear-fed anger in the Yard and the Divisions.

And there was Ruth.

She had been taken to her flat by her solicitor. Sol Klein had been at Wilmington Court to welcome her. Two policemen would now watch the flats by day and by night.

Hann-Gorlay recovered consciousness during the night, but was still too ill to be questioned; there was little to ask him at this juncture. Roger toyed with the idea that the M.P. and Ruth were involved together, but the deeper he probed, the more he convinced himself that Hann-Gorlay was too wealthy to be a reasonable suspect.

It had always been easy to conjure up mind pictures of Ruth. It was as easy to recall the way she and Hann-Gorlay had behaved the previous night. There hadn't seemed any doubt that they were desperately, hopelessly in love. That seemed to be the only thing bringing them together. If Ruth were concerned with the robberies and the violence against the police, would she go with the man who was leading a campaign against them?

She might—

But could she show so convincingly that she was in love with the man, if she were fooling him?

Sloan and Roger were in Roger's office when the

door opened and Chatworth made one of his rare visits.

It was half-past three on the day of the remand.

Both men stood up. Chatworth waved them back to their chairs, and dropped into one himself.

"Expect this Linder woman to jump bail, Roger?"

"I've an open mind."

"What would it profit her, if she did?"

Roger shrugged. "She might hope to get overseas safely. I've checked, and can't trace that she has any contacts abroad. She's never kept in touch with relatives anywhere, as far as I've been able to find out. But even if she tries to jump bail, I think we'll hold her all right." He smiled faintly. "If she tries, she'll be telling the world that she's guilty—that's the most likely deterrent."

"Sure about this charge?"

Roger said, "We can prove she had stolen goods in her possession, and I don't think any jury would believe that she didn't know about it. We can prove that several of her boy friends also had stolen goods. We can show that she was a friend of Mortimer's and Gedd's, and even if they won't give evidence against her—Mortimer might, if he thinks Queen's Evidence would help him—I think we can persuade the jury that she's as guilty as hell."

"D'you think she is?" rumbled Chatworth.

"I haven't any reason to think that she isn't."

Chatworth grunted.

"Well, you know what you're doing. Made a close study of the newspapers today?" His grin was almost ferocious. "Apart from the congratulations which they shower on you, what do you think of them?"

"They're going to have this Citizens' League built up into a gigantic vigilante organization before we know where we are," said Roger. "If they start carrying arms, I think we're going to run right into trouble. We could stop them from using guns, but not cudgels."

"Has the fellow we caught at the Albert Hall said anything?"

"Not a word, yet. I can't find that he's a member of a big gang. He has one or two friends; they've pulled off a job or two and picked up guns. They're like the rest of 'em—desperadoes without any moral values at all; boys gone bad. But they are *not* all members of an big organization. I—" The telephone bell rang. "Excuse me, sir." He lifted the receiver. "Hallo?"

He listened—and his eyes glinted, his whole face lit up.

"Fine!" he exclaimed. "I'll be right over." He jumped up. "Randall says he'll talk—that's the Albert Hall gunman. I'm going over to him right away."

"Where is he?"

"St. Thomas's," Roger said. "We've almost taken control of the hospital!" The way he spoke betrayed the intensity of his hopes.

Randall still looked very pale and shaken. His neck was badly bruised, and he moved it with difficulty. Words seemed to be painful to utter, too.

"Why did you shoot at Hann-Gorlay?" Roger asked mildly, as he sat by the side of the bed in a small ward.

Sloan was with him, open notebook in his hand.

"It's all very well for rich swine like that to shout

the odds," Randall muttered. "He's got everything. Why shouldn't others have some of it? I just—I just hated his guts."

There was a peculiar bitterness in his voice; it was as if he still felt able to justify himself.

"Have you used a gun before?"

"I've carried one several times, but hadn't had to use it," Randall said. He licked his lips. "But I would have, if anyone had got in my way. I might as well tell you the truth—I don't need telling that lying won't do me any good now." He gave a twisted grin. "I still wish I'd killed him."

"Well, you didn't, so you won't hang for that job," Roger said, briskly. "Where did you get the gun from?"

"Listen, West. Talking will make things easier for me, won't it? If I turn Queen's Evidence—"

"It'll make things easier," Roger said promptly. "Where did you get the gun?"

"I got it from Roy Prescott, weeks ago," Randall said. "I wouldn't squeal, only he's dead. He—*he* got guns from a man named Lamb. Told me about it one day when he was sozzled. Micky Lamb, in Chelsea...."

The news was like an eruption.

Lamb was Mortimer's bookmaker friend.

21

Micky Lamb

Micky Lamb ran his bookmaking business and a small secondhand shop in a side street off the King's Road, Chelsea, not far from the Chelsea Town Hall. It was an excellent residential neighborhood, all the houses were solid, and Micky Lamb, whose name was on the fascia board above the shop, had a good-class business. He even sold *objets d'art*, pictures and jewelry, although he touched little of any great value.

The police knew him well as a trader and bookie with a good reputation.

"Going to pick Lamb up?" Sloan asked hopefully.

"Not yet," Roger said. "We'll see what regular visitors he has. We should find some odds and ends about what he's been doing, soon—and from now on we'll watch him as closely as we'll watch Ruth. See if we can find a connection between Ruth and Lamb, too." He talked jerkily, his thoughts outrunning his words. "Just sit back and have him watched."

"What about Pauline Weston?" Sloan asked. "Still holding back from her?"

"For a bit longer."

Sloan said, "I hope nothing crazy happens in the next day or two." He obviously wasn't pleased.

"We just have to hold our breath," Roger said. "I can use a bit of time. I'm going to see whether Gedd or Mortimer can tell us any more about Micky Lamb."

"All right," Sloan said. "But, Roger..." He stood up, no longer looking boyish, but very grim and mature. "I'm usually with you all the way. I'm not so sure that I am, this time. You're letting Lamb and Pauline Weston ride—and they may be planning another vicious attack."

Roger said slowly, "We're not seeing eye to eye over this job at all, Bill, but it will come right."

He hoped it would come right.

Gedd and Mortimer swore that they knew Micky Lamb only as a bookmaker. Roger couldn't prove that they were lying.

Ruth Linder did not appear to have had any business with the Chelsea secondhand dealer. Brammer swore that he hadn't met or heard of Lamb. It was Peel, probing as conscientiously as ever, who discovered from a Chelsea policeman that Lamb had a lot of young clients, and occasionally had visits from a girl who came in a red Morris Minor.

This time Roger saw Pauline at her flat. She wore a two-piece suit of cherry red and a white blouse. She looked fresh and calm—that calmness, a kind of serenity, was the most remarkable thing about her.

"I've been to Lamb's shop because I've bought a few oddments from him—that cigarette box, for instance." She pointed to a carved wooden box, probably East African. "That's all."

"Did you ever sell him stolen jewels?"

"I've never had any."

"Do you object to having your flat searched?"

"Not at all, if you think it necessary."

"That's fine," said Roger. "I do."

He and Peel went through the flat, and found nothing at all that helped. The girl seemed indifferent, remained courteous, and politely saw them out.

Reports from the Chelsea police and from Peel made a pretty clear picture. Many of Micky Lamb's customers—he called them clients—were young fellows. The local police had thought nothing of that; youngsters did bet heavily. Young men bought presents, too. Why not? But when the full reports were in, it was obvious that the number of young men who called on Micky Lamb was surprising.

Some called after dark, at the flat above his shop where he lived with his wife.

On the second day after Randall had named Micky lamb, more youths than usual called at the shop. Peel sent urgently for help, and each youth was followed when he left Lamb. Some arrived on foot, some on motorcycle, two or three in cars. There were nine, all together. Each of them lived in southwest London.

Every movement they made was watched for the rest of the day.

As dusk fell, Roger and Sloan pulled up in a car outside a café in Kensington where one of the youths was having a meal. This one was named Hargreaves. The two Yard men went in. Hargreaves was sitting alone at a table. He was well dressed, twenty or twenty-one, with a thin, nasty-looking mouth. He glanced up at the newcomers, and then went on with his meal.

Roger ordered a cup of tea, and took it to Hargreaves's table.

He sat down.

Hargreaves put his knife and fork down, and slid his right hand toward his pocket. Behind him, Sloan moved slowly, stealthily.

"No need to crowd me," Hargreaves said, thinly.

"Two's not a crowd," Roger said. "Mind telling me why you went to Micky Lamb this afternoon?"

Hargreaves had bright little brown eyes. His hand crept into his pocket, and his whole body tensed.

"To place a bet. That's my business, anyway," he said. "Who're you?"

"I'm a police officer, and—"

Hargreaves snatched his hand from his pocket, with a gun in it. Sloan swung his arm and caught the youth a flat-handed blow on the side of the face. The gun barked. A girl behind the counter screamed, another clung to her companion.

Hargreaves crashed to the floor, falling with his chair, while Roger took his gun, and Sloan slipped on the handcuffs.

It was all over in three minutes.

There was a silent journey to the Yard.

They took the prisoner to a waiting room. He started off with a show of bravado, but it didn't last for long. Within ten minutes he was confessing that he had planned to break into a house that night, that he had got the gun from Micky Lamb, and knew others who often did the same. He worked for himself. He only stole money, wouldn't have anything to do with jewelry.

He said that he had never heard of Ruth Linder.

The call for the other youthful "customers" to be picked up went out as soon as Roger finished questioning Hargreaves. Squad cars quickly rounded them all up. Only one managed to get at his gun in time to use it, and he did no damage. Three were insolent and refused to talk; the others admitted that they had got the guns from Micky Lamb. By nine o'clock that night Roger knew how many crimes they had committed. Most of them stole only cash, a few took jewels. Micky Lamb bought these, at a low price, and expected a cut in the cash yield. He supplied guns, coshes, knuckle dusters—any kind of weapon.

They always had to return these next day.

There was a loosely organized gang, with Lamb the leader who took no active part; but he often told the youths of likely places to burgle.

There was a form of oath of secrecy; and Lamb held them down by threats of what would happen to them if they squealed. One or two, it was found, had been badly beaten up after showing signs of revolt.

None of the prisoners admitted having heard of Ruth Linder.

All of them showed something of the bitterness and the warped thinking of Gedd and Randall, Hann-Gorlay's assailant. It was a mixture of bravado and callousness, which Lamb had traded on.

"It isn't the big thing," Roger said to Sloan.

"We agree about that, anyhow," Sloan said dryly. "Supports your argument, doesn't it? That it's not a closely integrated gang."

"More or less," Roger agreed.

"I think that half of 'em would have stopped carrying guns if they'd thought they might meet a copper with one."

Roger forced a grin. "The other half would become more deadly, but we won't argue."

"Going to pick Lamb up?" Sloan asked; and obviously thought they should.

Roger said, "Let's see what he does when he realizes that he isn't going to get any of his guns back tomorrow. And let's see who else contacts him."

"All right," said Sloan, as if grudging his acquiescence. "There's one thing—we have picked up nine of the brutes. That ought to give Brammer and the Citizens' League a smack in the eye. I can't see many jobs being done tonight, either."

Roger didn't answer.

"Can you?"

Roger said, "Look at it this way, Bill. Every man we picked up lives in the southwest. What about the other districts of London? We could get a crop of trouble in those others. We'll alert all the Divisions outside of the southwest. If this is coordinated in any way, there'll be hell to pay in those districts tonight."

There were several burglaries in which the crooks were armed; one policeman, two night watchmen and a taxi driver were badly injured, two girls at a cinema pay box in the East End of London were coshed and a commissionaire badly injured in another raid. There were several more outrages that night than on average.

200

Two of the crooks were caught.

One was older than the youths the police had found before. The other was no more than twenty.

Neither of them admitted knowing Ruth Linder or Micky Lamb. The older man had a gun which he had picked up just after the war—a revolver. The youth had a .32 automatic. He said nothing, but Roger had his movements traced, and discovered that he often visited a shopkeeper in Bethnal Green, not far from Ruth's shop in the Mile End Road.

Under sharp questioning, the youth admitted that he got his gun from there.

When Roger had been called out to Putney, weeks ago, he had felt the sudden tension when the Yard had been geared to make a tremendous effort. He felt the same tension now—but the effort would be greater, and the stakes higher. Little had been said to anyone, but everyone seemed to sense that a crisis was coming—and that developments were beginning to favor the police.

With nine men due to appear before a magistrate that day, Roger had the shop in Bethnal Green covered. It was owned by a little man named Rickett, who ran a small jeweler's business, and whose reputation was excellent—nothing at all was known against him. But during the night the same facts had been discovered about Rickett as about Micky Lamb. He made book, and had a lot of young fellows among his customers—and several had called the previous afternoon and evening, many more than usual.

From ten past nine onward, the youths went back to the shop.

None stayed long.

Each was followed, and as soon as he was out of sight of Rickett's shop, was detained. The last called a little after eleven o'clock. Nothing else happened for an hour.

Roger and Sloan, who had been watching for two hours from a window in a flat opposite, went into the shop. Rickett was by himself. The shop was gloomy, nothing like so clean and attractive as that of Micky Lamb.

"Good morning, gentlemen." Rickett was a podge of a man, with a pale face and porcine eyes buried beneath the flesh. He smiled at them. He had moist lips, and spread his hands. "How can I help you?"

"You've had it, Rickett," Roger said. "We've come for the guns."

"I—I don't understand, sir, I—"

"And everything else they've brought back to you this morning," Roger said, and lifted a flap in the counter. "Mind if we come through?"

"Yes, I do mind! I protest—"

"Tell the beak about it," Roger said.

They found a small arsenal in a packing case behind the shop. There were twenty-nine automatic pistols, mostly .32's, and dozens of coshes, knuckle dusters and knives. In a safe they found a lot of stolen jewelry, some in its setting, some taken out. There was a small furnace oven for melting down gold.

Roger brought one of the youths—the one who seemed most likely to speak—and questioned him in Rickett's presence. Between them, they told a convincing story. Rickett ran a loosely integrated organization, youths formed a kind of secret soci-

202

ety, and the weak ones were beaten up. Another thing came out: any youth caught by the police was primed with a phony story about where he'd obtained his weapons.

"Do you work with Micky Lamb of Chelsea?" Roger asked Rickett.

"Micky who?"

"Lamb."

"I have never heard of such a man," Rickett said earnestly. "I wouldn't have started all this, but I had to. I—"

Roger grinned, skeptically.

"But it's true! The bitch of a woman ..."

"What woman?" Roger flashed.

"She has been visiting me for two years now," Rickett told him viciously. "Always by night, so I can never see her face. She—she blackmailed me—"

"How?"

"She knew I sometimes bought a few hot jewels to help some poor fellow out," Rickett muttered. "Now I have to give her a share of my proceeds, West. She started the gun business, made me get the kids together. If I'd refused she would have given me away."

"Just a woman?" Roger rapped.

"Yes. Yes. I—"

"Who else?"

"It's always the woman, she—"

"Listen," Roger said. "You'd follow her and knock her on the head if you thought she was in this by herself. Who's behind her?"

Rickett muttered, "I don't know. I've followed her twice, and each time a couple of men attacked me. Why, they nearly beat my brains out! And the second time my shop was raided, the furniture was smashed up. I—I did what she told me after that."

"And you don't know her?"

"Not from Adam!"

"What about Ruth Linder?"

"Uncle Benny's girl? No, it—it can't be Ruth. She wouldn't—" Rickett broke off, as if uncertain of himself. "Could have been, I suppose, but I can't be sure. This bitch always wears a big raincoat, and a floppy hat—oh, and a big veil. I shouldn't think it was Ruth, though. Too tall."

Roger took out a photograph of Pauline Weston.

"Shouldn't think it was her, either," Rickett muttered, "but I can't be sure."

Roger said: "All right, but try to remember something about the woman. Where did you get your guns?"

"Picked up one here, another there." Rickett licked his lips.

"Why always .32's?"

"They're easier to carry and it's simple to get ammunition for one size."

That was reasonable.

After it, Roger rammed home question after question, until he felt sure that a cringing, exhausted Rickett couldn't tell him another thing. The man was pathetic.

"Take him to Cannon Row, Bill," Roger said. "I'll see you at the Yard."

Half an hour later he was in his office, beginning to feel excited. The first crack had come, and was a big one. The statements were fitting in with his own theories, always good for morale. The story of the woman blackmailer sounded exactly what he wanted to hear; could point at Ruth, too. He'd tackle Lamb, soon, or else Sloan would go crazy.

He wished he and Sloan weren't differing so much.

He could see Sloan's point of view; it was simply a matter of disagreement. Sloan believed in the lash, and would feel safer if he carried a gun. Who could blame him? A policeman was a policeman, not a social reformer.

The telephone bell rang.

"Sergeant Peel for you, sir," the operator said.

Peel was watching Micky Lamb's shop.

"Put him through." Roger was eager. "Hallo... hallo, Jim. Any luck?"

"Pauline Weston's just gone in to see Lamb," Peel said.

22

Night of Terror

Pauline's now black Morris Minor was parked outside Micky Lamb's shop.

Roger drove past, with Sloan beside him. Peel was at a corner not far along the street, and other police were watching. Peel came up as they turned the corner and slowed down. His eyes were shiny with anticipation. The feeling that they were nearing the end was in him as it was in most of them—a kind of repressed excitement.

"She's still there."

"Anyone else with them?" asked Roger.

"No—expect anyone else?"

"I'd like to be sure," Roger said. "When Pauline leaves, you follow her. I'll go and see Micky."

Peel didn't actually say it, but looked as if he thought: "Not before it's time."

Peel moved away from the car and glanced along the street. Roger and Peel got out. They hadn't been there for more than five minutes before Brammer's girl friend left the secondhand shop. She looked pale—but, then, she always did. She did not look about her, or appear to wonder whether she was watched; she was perfectly self-possessed.

Peel was soon after her, in an M.G.

"Now for Micky," Sloan said.

Roger grinned. "At last!"

They knew what Micky Lamb was like—a tall, aristocratic-looking man with iron-gray hair, a courtly manner and extremely good looks.

He was in the shop with his wife, an overripe Juno of a woman, when Roger and Sloan entered. He glanced at them quickly, and Roger sensed that he had recognized them as police. He smiled and moved toward the back of the shop, with a word of apology, and said:

"Come and see what I have here, my dear."

His wife followed him.

Roger let them both disappear, then went after them.

Micky Lamb was hurrying toward a door which led into a back yard, and to an alley leading to the main road.

"I shouldn't, Lamb," Roger said. "We want a little chat with you."

Lamb was in the doorway. The yard, and the illusion of freedom, were in front of him. His right hand was at his pocket. There was another, curious illusion—that the man was in face much younger than his years. He reminded Roger of all the youths who had been arrested—had the same defiant, sneering manner.

"Don't be a fool," Roger went on. "The shop is covered, back and front."

"Micky, listen." The Junoesque woman's voice was hoarse and her eyes were frightened, as if the years had bred fear in her. "Micky, don't do anything silly; don't try to get away."

Roger drew nearer. His gun was handy but he didn't take it out. Sloan would expect him to—but oddly, it was because of Sloan that he felt that he had to handle this without one.

Micky Lamb's hand bunched in his pocket.

"If you use your gun," Roger said, "you'll get a hell of a long sentence." He held out his hand. "Give it to me."

Micky didn't speak.

"Micky," the woman repeated, in that entreating voice, "don't ask for trouble, don't—" She caught her breath.

A Chelsea man in uniform was turning into the yard.

There was a moment of tension, when it looked as if Micky Lamb might try to shoot his way free. Roger kept away from his own gun, still held his hands out; but he watched the bunched fist, ready to fling himself to one side.

"Roger, use—" Sloan began.

"Micky—" gasped the woman.

"Stop your damned bleating!" Micky Lamb snarled.

He moistened his lips, then took his hand out of his pocket—empty. In a flash, Roger and Sloan were alongside him.

Sloan took his gun away.

"That was sensible," Roger said. He felt vindicated, almost foolish. "Take it easy, Mrs. Lamb." He nodded to the Chelsea man to look after the woman. "Where do you keep the other stuff, Lamb?"

Lamb said, "Who squealed?"

"We reached you in the end. We always catch up."

"Who squealed?" asked Lamb again.

"Let's talk about it later," Roger said easily. "I've a search warrant, but you can save me a lot of trouble. Where's the stuff—the arsenal?"

"To hell with you," Lamb growled.

It was more bravado than anything else. The veneer of culture wasn't very thick, and his power of resistance was weak. He led the way upstairs. The store of guns, coshes and knuckle dusters were kept in an old oak coffer beneath his bedroom window. There was quite as much stuff as there had been at Rickett's place.

There was more stolen jewelry, too.

"Let's get this stuff checked as soon as we can," Roger said to Sloan. "See if it ties up with any of the stuff found at Ruth's place." This was while Micky Lamb was watching them at work. "Know Ruth Linder, Lamb?"

Lamb didn't speak.

"Did you know Uncle Benny?"

"Everyone knew Uncle Benny," Lamb said.

"Are you working with Ruth?"

Lamb didn't speak.

"Or Pauline?" Roger asked, smoothly.

Micky Lamb said viciously, "I don't know who she is. She comes here by night, hides her face—and puts the black on me. She made me start the arms racket, she—"

"Was it Pauline Weston? The girl who was here just now?"

Lamb looked startled.

"I—I don't know. She's been here as a customer lately, but the other one comes at night. She discovered I—I fenced a bit. Then she started putting on the black. I—I tried to find out who was behind her, followed her one night, and—look!"

Lamb thrust his left arm out and pulled up coat and shirt sleeve. A nasty scar, red and knotty, showed halfway up the forearm.

"Two men did that with a broken bottle. Another time they raided the shop, and nearly frightened my wife out of her wits. They actually stripped her, and—" Lamb broke off.

"So you sat back and took it," Roger sneered.

"I had to!"

"You made plenty," Roger said. "You don't regret—"

"Listen, West. Who squealed?" Lamb broke in viciously. *"Was it Brammer?"*

Lamb wouldn't say any more; except that he believed Brammer was in the game.

The man was held at Cannon Row that night. He refused to make another statement, but would probably change his mind. His wife was questioned while Roger went to his own office at the Yard.

The telephone rang while he was scanning reports.

"West speaking."

"It's Peel here," Peel said, and this time he sounded vitriolic. "I've lost Pauline Weston. She meant to give me the slip, and did it."

"I'll put a call out for sweet Pauline," Roger said softly.

*   *   *

An hour later he pulled his car up outside the Fleet Street offices of the *Courier*, but didn't get out immediately. He lit a cigarette. Two plain-clothes men, who had come on ahead of him, nodded as they passed.

He drew at the cigarette.

He could still remember the venom with which Lamb had flung out that question: *"Was it Brammer?"* Not long before, Pauline Weston had talked to Lamb, and then driven off in the car which had been used in Roger's kidnaping.

Ruth Linder had accused Brammer of stirring up the trouble.

The one thing which cut across the theory that Brammer was in it, if not behind it, was the fact that he had talked of Pauline's once-red Morris Minor. For the rest, Brammer fitted. If Brammer were behind, or even associated with a lot of brutal young criminals, it would have been easy for one of them to have put the stolen jewels in Ruth's room. Brammer could have fixed it, but—why? The obvious argument against it, the thing which made it appear illogical, was the fact that Brammer was more responsible than any one else for the uprising against the crimes of violence.

But if he wanted to make the task of the police almost impossible, surely this was a way: the League, any corps of vigilantes, would incite the criminals to greater violence, and give the police a fantastic task.

Logic mattered; but Lamb's venom when he had spat out that question seemed to matter just as much.

211

"Was it Brammer?"

Roger got out of the car, dropped his cigarette and stamped it out, and went into the main entrance of the *Courier*. It was a palatial place of shiny walnut veneer and chromium furniture and fittings and four lifts.

Brammer's office was on the third floor.

Roger didn't ask for Brammer, but went straight to the office. He didn't want to give the man a moment's warning. He wasn't sure that it was the time to accuse Brammer. He wasn't sure about anything. Ruth was under charge for free—and if she were guilty, responsible for a blunder that it was hard to believe she had really committed. Overconfidence might explain the jewels at the flat, but—

Roger tapped at the door of an office which was marked *J. K. Brammer—Private*, then opened it and stepped inside. Brammer's secretary, a skinny girl with a lean, sallow face and an air of permanent surprise, told him that Brammer was out.

"But Mr. Matthewson is here, sir."

"I'll see him, please," Roger said.

Rodney Matthewson was at a desk in Brammer's office. He took off his pince-nez, and stood up promptly.

"Why, Mr. West. I'm working on some plans for our next meetings. I hope you'll be glad; things are going extremely well." When Roger didn't answer, Matthewson went on, "How are you?"

"Worried," Roger said. This wasn't the time to talk about the League or tell Matthewson what he thought of inciting desperadoes to greater violence. Matthewson, Hann-Gorlay, Brammer—all of them would disagree with that anyway. "I want to see Brammer, urgently."

"He left only an hour or so ago," Matthewson told him. "He said that Pauline was anxious to see him." Matthewson looked troubled. "I know he's been worried about some of her friends, Mr. West, but I can't believe that Pauline—"

He broke off.

"I hope you're right," Roger said gruffly. "If Brammer comes in, ask him to call me, will you?"

"Immediately, Mr. West."

"Thanks."

Roger went out. The worried face of the solicitor stayed in his mind's eye. Had Matthewson already considered the possibility that Brammer was involved?

Downstairs, Roger telephoned the Yard from a call box in the main office. Sloan told him that Brammer hadn't been reported from Wilmington Place or anywhere else connected with the affair. Ruth had spent an hour at the hospital with Hann-Gorlay, and was back at her flat.

"Put a general call out for Brammer," Roger said. "Don't have him brought in—we just want to know where he is."

"Okay."

"Anything else turned up there?"

Sloan chuckled.

"Chatworth's like a dog with two tails. We've pulled in seventeen youngsters known to handle guns, as well as Micky Lamb and Rickett. Chatworth thinks that we're really getting to the end of it. He's sent a special chit to the Back Room Inspector—when the Press come round, he wants them to spread these 'achievements of the Yard' far and wide." Sloan chuckled again. "And is he pleased with Roger West!"

Sloan's voice had lost that echo of censure, too.

"Well, who's complaining?" Roger asked.

He rang off, and went into the street. One of the Yard men strolled past him.

"Watch and follow Brammer's secretary," West said out of the corner of his mouth, and the other gave an almost imperceptible nod.

Roger got into the car.

He ought to be feeling as cheerful as Chatworth. It was the first time since the wave of violence had started that the police could show really big results. He didn't doubt that every policeman, from the lowliest copper on the beat up to Chatworth, was feeling as if the long run of failure was near its end.

Ought he to feel the same?

Whatever he ought to feel, he felt depressed, almost dejected. Was it Ruth or was it Pauline and Brammer? How far did the campaign go, as a campaign? By now the newspapers had carried the story of the morning arrests, and news would have spread fast through the East End and wherever the youths foregathered.

There had been reprisals against Hann-Gorlay at the Albert Hall.

Would there be more?

Rodney Matthewson usually reached his Surbiton home about seven o'clock in the evening. He caught the same train each evening, unless he were going to a special meeting.

He had none to attend that night.

He lived near the station, and although he sometimes went home by taxi, he often walked on clear, crisp nights. He did now. Soon after he turned off the High Street, one of the local policemen recognized him. They were near Matthewson's house, and walked together. They agreed about the weather and the "bad business" of armed violence.

"How's your campaign going, sir?" the constable asked.

"Very well, I think, very well." Matthewson glanced up at a heavy face. "What do you think about being armed, Smith?"

"It's not for me to say, sir."

"Very tactful of you," smiled Matthewson. "You're wise."

They reached his gate.

The policeman saw nothing, but Matthewson stopped suddenly, and caught his breath.

"Constable, who—"

He saw a dark figure, and leaped to one side. The figure, of a youth, came from Matthewson's front garden.

He fired three shots.

The policeman made an odd, choking sound.

Matthewson fell to the ground, but wasn't hurt. The echo of the shots was still in his ears when a car turned into the street, and the gunman turned and raced toward a motorcycle. He had disappeared before Matthewson got to his feet.

The constable was dead.

Ralph Kenworthy, a Citizens' League man of whom Matthewson and Hann-Gorlay had great hopes, always used his car to drive from his home in Hampstead, for his business took him about London a great deal, and a car was still the quickest and the cheapest means of transport. As he turned into his drive, the gates of which stood open, he was thinking that he must have a word with Matthewson on the telephone. That could come after dinner. He saw the light on in the front room. Mary, his wife, would be putting out the whisky and soda.

The garage doors were also standing open.

He drove the car straight in, then got out slowly, closed the garage doors and turned the key in the padlock.

He heard a slight sound behind him, but before he could turn, a blow crashed onto the back of his head.

He dropped down, groaning.

Another blow fell—another and another.

He didn't see the front door open, light stream out, or his wife run, screaming. He didn't see the two youths who had attacked him rush at his wife, knock her down, kick her viciously—and run off only when neighbors rushed out, alarmed by her screams.

Roger was at Bell Street, with Janet, and the boys were doing their homework, when the report about Matthewson came through. He had hardly rung off before he was called again and told about Kenworthy, who wasn't dead but was in a pitiful state.

"I'm sorry, folks," he said; "I'll have to go to the Yard."

Janet was too affected by his expression to protest. If she hadn't reminded him, he would have forgotten to say good night to the boys. The boys stared....

Roger watched the shadowy doorways of Bell

Street; and cars parked just round the corner in King's Road, and his nerves were as taut as they had ever been again. Once in the main road, he drove fast; he was at the Yard in less than fifteen minutes.

Three more reports of attacks on officials of the Citizens' League had come in.

Within an hour, all but three of the branches were affected. There were three murders; the others were coshings and beatings-up, most of them resulting in grave injuries.

Sloan, who had also rushed back to the Yard, said grimly:

"Brammer and Pauline Weston are missing, and Ruth hasn't stirred from her flat since she went to see Hann-Gorlay."

217

23

The Raid

The news of the outrages burst upon London through the newspapers next morning, and spread like a fire through the city of millions. Before, the people had been shocked and shaken. Now, they were outraged and angry. There had been anger at the Albert Hall, at meetings everywhere—the kind of anger which had turned two ordinary, decent little men into would-be killers of the youth who had shot at Hann-Gorlay. This was worse.

The *Courier* filled its front page with the story.

Here was a challenge which had to be taken up. The successes that the Yard had had were almost wiped out in the public mind. Those leaders of the Citizens' League who had escaped, and others who quickly replaced them, called for a single devastating attack against the criminals. By midday meetings were taking place at Hyde Park and Tower Hill and in many of the other parks and open spaces, not often used for soapbox orators; and there was only one subject.

At Parliament Square a meeting of several thousand people held up the traffic, and an elderly, white-haired man with a golden voice called for a monster petition to Parliament—carrying the signatures of millions.

"And what do we do?" Sloan asked, as he went back to the Yard after looking at the surging crowd. "Send a call out for Brammer, watch Ruth Linder, hunt for Pauline Weston. This is organization with a capital O. It's a terror campaign, with one big mind behind it."

"All right," said Roger. "But Lamb doesn't know Rickett, Rickett doesn't know Lamb. Each had a gang of sorts, but the two gangs didn't work together. The only connecting factor is this mysterious woman blackmailer. We can't prove that it's Ruth—or that it's Pauline. The fact that Brammer went to see Pauline and disappeared could point to her, but it's only a pointer. We can't blame anyone for getting sore at us."

"When you stop to think," Sloan said, "we can't blame anyone for this vigilante idea, either. There were *fourteen* attacks last night. And what have we done?"

That tension of constraint was back.

"Where's the map?" Roger asked, and spread a big map of London over the desk. "We picked up Lamb in Chelsea and Rickett in Bethnal Green. If we divide London into areas of eight, that leaves six. I think we'll eventually find at least six more of these swine holding the arsenals—six more Lambs or Ricketts. *They* may be organized—they may be operating under the orders of this same mysterious woman. They're buying stuff from these kid gangsters. They've got a kind of dynamite to play with—imagine Rickett or Lamb dishing out guns to their customers, with a casual:

'Why not have a go at So-and-so tonight?'—at Matthewson, for instance, or Kenworthy. Or a copper. That's the way it could be done."

Sloan said, "You still mean it's inspired rather than directed?"

"Yes, Bill. Oh, there's a gang. The gang that kidnaped me, that sent the letter threats, other things —these crimes are not the work of one Londonwide network."

"I hope you're right," Sloan said.

"The vital thing is to pick Brammer and Pauline up soon," Roger went on.

"Every copper in London's on the lookout for them," Sloan said exasperatedly. "I—"

The telephone bell rang.

It was Peel.

"We've got Pauline Weston," he said. "We've got her where she can't get away, anyhow. In ..."

It was a house standing in its own grounds in Wimbledon, used as a Youth Club. Lights blazed from the windows, and shone on grass lawns, on shrubs and drives. The police were still at the walls and at the gates. Two uniformed men who had started to go in had been shot, but not seriously injured.

Peel told Roger and Sloan this as they got out of Roger's car. From the crowd which had gathered and was being held back by uniformed police, people called out:

"There's West."

"Who else is inside?" West demanded.

"I can't be sure," said Peel. "I had a radio message that Pauline Weston had turned up here. A constable on the beat saw and recognized her. He's watched this house for the past day or two; it's used as a club by youngsters—Randall used to come."

Roger nodded approval and understanding.

"Pauline drove in, a kid opened the door, and Pauline went straight in," Peel said. "Her car's just outside the front door now. The constable sent for help at once. Two of our chaps went up to the house, another stayed at the gates. They were shot at."

"What's happened since?"

Roger lit a cigarette, cupping his hands round the match to prevent the light from showing too clearly.

"Not much," Peel said. "The house is completely surrounded now; they can't get out."

"And Pauline went there willingly—freely, any-how?"

"No doubt about that."

"Any word of Brammer?"

"No."

Roger hesitated, drew at his cigarette, and said slowly:

"I'd better go and talk to them."

"It's not so simple as that," Sloan protested. "We need an armored car. That'll get us up to the door. There's no need to ask for trouble."

Roger didn't speak.

"Don't keep making a ruddy hero out of your-self!" Sloan burst out.

Roger spun round. Anger surged; he had never felt like this with Sloan before, and he could have knocked him down. Peel opened his mouth to speak again, and closed it like a trap. Sloan real-ized what he had set off, and began to speak:

"You know what I mean, I don't want you killed."

It was halting, uncertain.

A car turned into the street, the horn suddenly blaring out. It was an excuse for Roger to look away from Sloan. As he moved, he realized that he was far too edgy, his nerves were red raw.

The car had stopped abruptly. Police hurried toward it, and the crowd surged away. Apparently on police orders, the headlights were switched out. Soon the driver and the passengers were visible beneath a street lamp.

Ruth Linder and Sol Klein had arrived.

As soon as he recognized Ruth, Roger hurried forward. Another car turned into the street; the Yard men watching Ruth hadn't been far behind.

Ruth was getting out of the car.

"Fancy meeting you," Roger said bitingly. "Come to see some friends?"

"What's happening here?" She was aloof, almost indifferent to him, and tried to look beyond the gates of the house.

"We've trapped some gunmen in there."

Ruth didn't speak.

"What brought you?" Roger demanded.

She still didn't speak, but looked at Sol Klein. He was flabby, bright-eyed and nervous, and his lips were working.

"Ruth, we shouldn't have come; I told you we shouldn't have come, Ruth." He was clutching her arm. "We must get away from here; it's silly to stay."

"Why did you come?" Roger demanded roughly.

Sol raised his hands, rolled his eyes and looked as if appealing to the heavens for the right words.

"It was a telephone call," he said thickly. "Pauline Weston promised to give Ruth proof that those jewels had been planted at her flat. Such a story! I told her not to come, I *begged* her not to."

"So Pauline said that?" Roger sneered at Ruth.

She flashed her lovely eyes at him.

"I told you from the beginning that she and Brammer were behind this, didn't I?"

"If you thought that, why did you fall for this?"

Ruth said bitterly, "Unless I can prove that someone else planted those jewels at my flat, I shall spend the next few years in jail. That's how my uncle began—*he* was framed. If I ever went to prison, you'd never let me have any peace afterward. You police are—"

"Ruth, don't; Ruth, keep quiet!" Sol begged. "That talk won't do any good; it just won't do any good."

Ruth set her lips, tightly.

"We'll talk later," Roger said, and went back to his car. Peel and Sloan were by his side. "Bill," he added, and his voice was very calm, with no hint of anger, "I think this setup stinks. Send for that armored car, get it up as quickly as you can."

He opened the door of his own car and climbed in.

"What are you going to do?" Sloan demanded.

"I'm going to get inside that house. I don't think we've time to wait."

"You're an obstinate, thick-skinned idiot," growled Sloan in a voice which didn't carry. "I'll come with you."

"You stay here," Roger said. "That's an order."

"Let me—" Peel began.

"Give me ten minutes at least, then come if you think you should," Roger said.

He started the engine.

Silence fell upon the crowd as they realized what he was going to do. He didn't waste time. He kept on the sidelights but didn't use the head-lamps; that would have given the men at the house a split second of extra warning.

He rammed his foot on the accelerator and raced toward the house: he was halfway along the drive when a bullet shattered the windscreen. He flinched, but wasn't touched. He switched on the headlights, could just see the little black Morris, swerved past it and crashed into the wall of the house. He was ready for that, and took the shock of the crash, then thrust a door open and jumped out.

24

Brammer

Brammer lay on the floor of an upstairs room at the house with his wrists tied behind his back. The door was open, and every now and again a youth looked in.

Sometimes Pauline Weston came, but she never stayed long and was never alone.

Youths walked about upstairs and down. Brammer could hear them talking; now and again there was an outburst of laughter. There was something false and strained about the attitude of the youths —a desperation which told that they knew they hadn't a chance now.

One of them came in, short, sallow, cigarette sticking out of his mouth, a gun in his hand. Another, taller youth joined him.

Brammer said savagely, "What the hell are you going to do?"

"Like to know, wouldn't you?" The short youth moved across and kicked him. It could have been much more vicious; as it was, he seemed to get a sadistic pleasure out of it. "You'll find out."

Pauline came in again. She wore a tailored gray

suit, was smoking and looked completely self-possessed. Brammer's eyes seemed tormented whenever he saw her.

The youth laughed, and moved back, then sauntered toward the door.

The taller youth said: "Like to know what we're going to do, Brammer?"

Brammer didn't speak.

"Because I'll enjoy telling you," the youth sneered. "We're going to shoot you. It's going to be suicide, see. We're going to fix you good and proper. If you'd care to know why, I'll tell you. It's because you've worked up this campaign against us. We're going to make you taste what it's like."

Brammer burst out, "What the hell are you waiting for? Get it over."

"It won't be long. We're going to have a conference, and then—"

He stopped.

A sound came from outside; a moment later a man inside the house shouted. The roar of the engine grew very loud, and shots cracked out from other rooms.

The youth strode to the window, kept to one side and thrust his gun forward—but he didn't shoot.

The car crashed, and glass splintered. The youth at the window spun around, white-faced. Then the engines of other cars started up. More shots rang out, but the cars didn't stop until they reached the house.

"That's curtains for you, Brammer," the youth said viciously; "we won't have time—"

"*You* won't have time," Pauline Weston said.

The youth looked stupefied.

Into Brammer's eyes there sprang a fierce, bright light.

Pauline snatched a small gun from her pocket and shot the youth in the arm. Then she raced across to the door, and slammed it, turned the lock, and spun round in time to stop the youth from rushing at her.

"Stay just where you are!"

He stood swaying on his feet, blood dripping from the wound in his arm.

Pauline backed toward Brammer.

"The police are here," she said, as if she hardly knew what she was talking about. "It's all right, my darling, it's all right. I got in with the brutes; to fool them I had to fool you. I hoped that I'd be able to prove who—"

She stopped.

Shooting crackled on the stairs and on the landing, but after a few tense minutes, it was quiet. Heavy footsteps sounded. They heard Roger West's voice. He reached the door and turned the handle.

He called, "Bill, this one's locked. Better becareful."

"It's all right," Pauline said.

She didn't call out loud enough for Roger to hear. Now that it was over, she was trembling, and her voice wouldn't keep steady. Her hand quivered as she unlocked the door.

"It's all right," she repeated. "Look—look what they were doing to him." She turned toward Brammer. "They intended to make it seem as if he committed suicide. That was going to 'prove' he

227

was the leader, but he isn't, I swear he isn't; he's nothing to do with it. Ruth—Ruth Linder is."

Roger bent over Brammer, untying the cord at his wrist. They hadn't been tied really tightly, and this could be as phony as anything that had gone before it.

"Now we'll have the proof," Roger growled.

"Ruth will soon be here, if she isn't already," Pauline said. "She phoned one of the boys, to say she was coming. She wanted to see Bram before he was killed. She was on the way, so couldn't be warned when you began the attack."

That might be true. Faced with the emergency outside, Ruth would have thought up a lie in a hurry.

"I still want proof," Roger said.

"We heard them talking," Brammer told him gruffly. "Oh, I know it won't give you any excuse to act, but it's true, Handsome. Pauline—"

"That's right," Roger said. "Let's hear what Pauline's been doing."

"Very well," Pauline said quietly. "I'll tell you. First of all, it began because Roy Prescott was my brother."

Roger felt as if she had kicked him. Brammer drew in a hissing breath. The girl looked at Roger all the time, silent while he absorbed the shock. Then, as if to thrust it further home, she went on:

"Long before the Putney murder, and before he was killed in the hospital, he had changed his name. I knew he had gone off the rails, that's why I got mixed up in it as soon as I could. I didn't know how far he'd gone, but I tried to make friends with some of his friends. I was sure he was under the influence of someone bad—probably a woman who was no good for him—with whom he was infatuated. He was as closed as an oyster, so I mixed with his friends, and pretended I liked them, so as to find out all I could. Mortimer seemed most likely, and I concentrated on him. I wanted to get at the woman before it *was* too late.

"Well, it was too late. Roy killed, and was killed, and I'd failed. I hadn't been able to help him after all. But—call it revenge if you like"—she looked at West defiantly—"I was determined to make someone pay for it. I like to think it wasn't just revenge, that I believed I could save other boys from going the same way as Roy, who was my younger brother. Take it how you like."

"Go on." Roger's voice was flat.

"Mortimer made it easier by falling in love with me. Easier in some ways, though embarrassing at times, as I had to hold him." Pauline shot a quick look at Brammer, but he did not meet her eyes. "I was prepared to suspect anyone and everyone. It wasn't long before I wondered about Bram. I wasn't sure that he was just a private eye. Even— even after I'd fallen in love with him, I had doubts. I meant to wait until I was sure, then tell him what I was doing, but—"

Pauline broke off.

"My God!" breathed Brammer. "And I thought you—" He paused, and glared at Roger.

"Since you had this information, why didn't you tell the police?" Roger asked. "Or did you suspect us, too?" That was almost a sneer.

Brammer went red.

Pauline said coolly, "I believed that if I waited until the last moment, it would be better. If I were ever in acute danger, I meant to come to you. But I didn't want to lose ground by asking for help too soon."

Roger said, "Why did you warn Mortimer about that brooch?"

"To convince him that I was on the level. I had to do things like that. And I let him use my car—"

"I suppose you know that he used the car to decoy me," Roger broke in sharply.

"That wasn't Mortimer," she said emphatically. "Someone else took the car—on Ruth Linder's orders, so as to implicate me. She knew I was checking on her by then." The girl sounded very tired.

"Why did you have it repainted black immediately afterward?"

"Mortimer told me to. He found out it had been used to frame me and was furious—and scared. He said I must have it painted, or the police would get me. I did what he told me, that's all."

"Was Mortimer your only real contact with the gang?"

"There was one other—Micky Lamb. I had followed Roy to the secondhand shop once or twice, and once Lamb called at Roy's flat when I was there. They were together a lot. I've been following that up too." Suddenly all the life went out of Pauline's voice. "That's all, I think," she said.

"You haven't told me how you got here," Roger reminded her.

"That—that won't take long." She forced herself to go on. "When Bram disappeared for the second time I took my one chance, and persuaded one or two of the boys that I was actually in the game.

They brought me here. At least I was able to stop them shooting Bram."

"How much of all this had you told Bram?" Roger asked.

"Nothing," Brammer growled. "I got onto Lamb myself, though. I was coming to tell you, but was shanghaied on the way."

"Lamb can't help us," said Roger, fighting back a heavy sense of disappointment. "He doesn't know much."

"Oh, yes, he does," said Pauline sharply. "So does his wife. I've seen her with Ruth."

"You have?" Roger's voice sharpened. "Brammer, did you tell anyone you'd got onto Lamb?"

"Only Pauline, and she knew already, though she didn't let on." Brammer gave Pauline a smile that was almost radiant, then turned back to Roger. "Where do we go from here?"

"You can both go home," said Roger. "Under escort," he added grimly. "I've plenty to do."

It was soon learned that Roger had been held prisoner in this house. In the back yard was timber and boards like that used in the crate.

One room was a kind of surgery, with a young medical student in charge. He dressed any wounds members of the gang might get. There were hypodermic syringes, morphia, a fairly complete first-aid unit. In another room there were crackmen's tools and two tubes of nitroglycerine.

Later, Roger and Sloan sat in Roger's office, with a silent Peel sitting on the arm of a chair near the fire. All three were smoking. Empty cocoa mugs and a plate with one curling sandwich were on Roger's desk.

231

It was after one in the morning.

"I still don't see where we go from here," Sloan said. "Both those girls' stories are as phony as hell. Suppose Pauline Weston is Roy Prescott's sister—and we can soon find out—how does that help?" He drew savagely at his cigarette. "She could still be in it up to her neck. *And* Ruth—which of them *is* fooling us? Who's the girl who blackmailed Micky Lamb and Rickett? Give Pauline a pair of falsies and Ruth some high heels, and they're much the same build. There isn't a hope of getting Lamb or Rickett to identify one or the other. Even if we tried, they'd give us a phony statement. Whoever's behind it set out to bamboozle us, and have they done a job!"

"Any ideas, Jim?" Roger asked Peel.

Peel shrugged. "No."

Roger said, "Well, I've got one, which might not amount to much. There's one man we've never paid much attention to. Sol Klein. He was nervous tonight, and didn't like Ruth being there at all. That might be normal, but could mean that he had special reason to feel nervous. Jim, you go and have a talk with Klein. Tackle him now that he's tired—wake him up, if necessary. Tell him that you've got the case against Ruth all sewn up. Tell him that we're going to hold her on another charge first thing in the morning, and she won't get a remand on this one. Tell him that we know he's in it, but if he'll talk, he may get off. Then come away."

"And you'll be waiting at Ruth's place," Peel said.

"If Klein convinces her that we're going to hold her, she may panic and run. It's worth trying,"

Roger added, "although she might guess that it's bluff."

Sol Klein hadn't gone to bed.

He saw Peel in the shop, hands trembling, wet lips quivering. Peel didn't know what he was talking about, Sol insisted; Ruth wasn't a criminal. He, Sol, hadn't done a dishonest thing in his life.

"I swear it, Sergeant, never once in my life—"

Peel laughed into his face.

"She'll drag you down with the rest of them, Sol. Tell us what you know about her."

"I don't know a thing!" Sol screeched.

Roger and Sloan were in a private car at a corner of Wilmington Place. Peel had sent word to the Yard and it had been passed on. There was no way of telling whether Sol Klein had taken any action. Certainly he hadn't visited Ruth. He might have telephoned; and if Peel had convinced him that it was desperate enough, might have persuaded Ruth to try to escape.

No policemen were in Wilmington Place itself, but one was at the window of a flat opposite, and could see the entrance of Ruth's block. The back exit was also covered. Police with walkie-talkie radio were stationed all round the block.

Everything was quiet for so long that Roger began to feel flat and jaded. Sloan was yawning, as if he couldn't keep his eyes open another minute. Dawn began to creep across the sky.

It wasn't going to work. If Ruth were guilty, she felt secure, and recognized the visit to Klein as a bluff. If she were innocent, then Brammer and Pauline—

233

The radio signal flashed.

Roger grabbed it. "Hallo?"

"She's left," he was told. "She's walking toward Park Lane."

"Fine! Keep close to her."

"She won't get away!"

Sloan was already starting the car, tiredness forgotten.

"On the move?"

"Toward Park Lane."

Sloan swung round two corners, then slowed down when they turned into Park Lane.

Ruth Linder had reached it and was walking toward Marble Arch. She knew that she was being followed; she must have known that for a long time. She almost certainly realized that if she wanted to escape from her shadowers, she would have to get among crowds.

Sloan drove slowly, two hundred yards ahead of her.

Another car came along at a sharp pace, then slowed suddenly alongside Ruth. Brakes squealed as it jolted to a standstill. There wasn't a chance to stop anything. Ruth jumped in, the door slammed, the car put on a furious burst of speed. A police whistle shrilled out.

Roger looked round desperately.

Sloan could see the headlights of the other car in his driving mirror. He pulled over, as if to let it go past. Its horn blared. He waited until the last moment, then wrenched his wheel. The driver of Ruth's car swung toward the pavement.

A shot flashed; the bullet passed in front of Sloan's face and went out by Roger's window. Another hit a tire, the wheel went wild in Sloan's hands.

The two cars collided, broadside on.

Ruth's car swayed wildly to one side, struck the curb, and looked as if it would turn over, then smacked into a lamppost.

As it did so, she opened the door and jumped out. Another car flashed along, one her rescuer had in reserve. Ruth raced toward it, and was inside before the police could get her. It drove on, scattering the police right and left.

The car was found abandoned, half a mile away. Ruth Linder and her rescuer had disappeared.

Back in Park Lane Roger recognized the woman driver of the first car which had come for Ruth.

It was Lamb's wife, badly injured.

Grimly, Roger started the hunt for Ruth and the driver, then went to see Mrs. Lamb. If she would talk—

She had died in the ambulance, and he was back where he started.

Roger went straight to Lamb, in his cell, told him about his wife and added simply that Ruth was on the run.

Lamb, who looked years older than he had, managed to sneer, "D'you think I'll fall for that crap?" But the bravado couldn't keep his fear away.

"You'd better come and see for yourself," Roger said.

He took Lamb to the morgue, under strong escort, and Lamb looked down on his wife's body.

For a few minutes he was shocked into silence. Then he began to tremble, soon he began to curse; after a while, the cursing ran into talking, into words which poured out.

Roger kept prompting him.

Lamb had been highly placed in the gang, and his story of an unknown woman blackmailer had been a blind.

"But Rickett told you the truth," he said flatly. "He doesn't know the woman was Ruth. Nor do the others . . ."

"Others?" said Roger, softly.

"There are eight of them, all bookies or junk dealers like me. They've all got an armory, they've been blackmailed by Ruth, but none of them knew who she was, I tell you. And they don't know who she works for any more than I do, unless—unless it was for some of her killer boyfriends."

"Think that's the answer?"

"No," said Lamb. "I don't think they've got the brains."

Roger switched: "Why pitch me that blackmail yarn?"

"I've told you, it was a blind, I tried to cover up. I knew that no one else could say anything different, they didn't know I was high up. So long as Ruth was free I was okay. At least, I had a chance."

Lamb had not wanted Ruth caught because she might think he had split, and take revenge by naming him in turn. He had named Brammer deliberately—as instructed to do by Ruth, if he were ever caught.

"But it doesn't matter now," he said brokenly. "You can have it all. If I knew who was behind Ruth, I'd tell you."

Lamb had been a major executive in the terror campaign. Acting under Ruth's instructions, he had sent the threatening letters, made the threatening phone calls—and arranged the unprovoked attacks on policemen. Those had been special jobs, done by specially chosen youths: desperate youths, who had been well paid for their work. They had all been sent out by Lamb, and were something apart from the ordinary armed robberies.

Lamb admitted that he had been close to Prescott, and that he had supplied Prescott with his private arsenal. He admitted also that he had arranged Prescott's murder at the hospital—again on Ruth's instructions.

"I don't know for certain why she wanted him croaked, but I think it was because he was getting too inquisitive. He told me he wasn't going to take orders from a woman much longer, said he'd been watching her, and believed he could name the man behind her. That was the last time I saw him alive."

"Sure there *is* someone behind her?" Roger asked.

Lamb said simply, "I know Ruth. She's got a lot of things that matter, but not the brains to organize this. Take that from me. She passed on orders, that's all."

"Hann-Gorlay's?"

"It could have been, I suppose," Lamb said. "There were a lot of kids who wouldn't know if he were on both sides of the fence."

"What about the nights when there was so much shooting?" Roger asked.

"Ruth gave the word," Lamb said. "Rickett and the others just had to spread the idea that it was a

237

night to let loose. If there were trouble in several places on the same night, it would set the police running round in circles. We dropped the idea in their minds, that's all. And I detailed the specials to attack the cops."

"What about the attacks on Matthewson and the leaders of the Citizens' League branches?"

"I don't know a thing," Lamb said. "Ruth told me to lay off the League—naturally enough, as she was mixed up in it. She told Rickett and the others the same, so those attacks weren't organized by us. But the kids we'd turned into gunmen wouldn't like the League boys. I couldn't understand why Ruth hobnobbed with them, but—" He shrugged. "She wasn't normal. She was eaten up with this hate complex against the police." He spoke as if she were already dead. "She didn't give a damn about danger—in fact I think she reveled in it."

Lamb's cigarette was finished, and he stubbed it out. Roger gave him another.

"Why did she release Brammer and me?"

"Oh, that job," Lamb said, and licked his lips. "She was going to bump you off. I had to detail one of the boys to borrow Pauline Weston's car when she wasn't looking—"

"Mortimer?"

"Not Mortimer. Fellow called Gedd. That part of it was to frame Pauline Weston, of course. We knew she was after us—she used to come nosing round the shop. It all went off all right, but when it was done it occurred to Ruth that it would make you look the biggest fool in England if you were released without being injured. The Yard would be at screaming point, so would your wife—and then the laugh would be on you. She hated you most,

238

West. She couldn't bear to have you killed, simply because then you wouldn't be there to hate." Lamb laughed shortly, unsteadily. "I don't know why she let Brammer go. He was getting pretty close to us."

Another thing Lamb did not know was why Mortimer and Gedd had raided Ruth's flat and shot Hann-Gorlay.

"Except that Mortimer may have been getting sweet on Pauline," he said as an afterthought. "And Ruth had it in for her."

Roger said slowly, "When did you get mixed up with her?"

"I knew her when she was a kid—just after her father was hanged and her mother committed suicide. Old Benny agreed with me, something happened to her then. She had started on this game before Uncle Benny died."

Lamb paused again.

Roger recalled how unsettled he had been about the killing of Old Benny; how he had suspected that he had never heard the whole truth.

"Go on."

Lamb said slowly, "Uncle Benny discovered that Ruth was working with another crook. He didn't like it, and said so. He said that if she didn't stop encouraging these kids to violence, he'd turn her over to the police. So she fixed her own uncle. She did it through Prescott—that was one of the reasons why he had to be rubbed out after he was caught. Prescott told young Harrock that Uncle Benny was going to put the police on him, and advised the boy what to do about it. Prescott was good at that sort of thing—he was an educated chap—and Harrock was easy to influence."

"So she would even do that," Roger said heavily.

239

"And still you'd work for her! What was in it for you, Lamb?"

"You'll find out when you search the shop, if you haven't already. I could have retired in another year. Ruth and the man behind her must make a fortune. Given time, they'd have been millionaires. Us fences bought from the boys, sold at a big profit—and split it with Ruth. If we got big stuff we always passed it on—Ruth's boss found a home for it. Give them their due, they paid us all a share. But we were the pawns, he was the King Fence. Call Ruth his Queen."

"Where is she now, Lamb?" Roger demanded.

"I don't know," Lamb said. "I just don't know."

No news came in about Ruth. Every newspaper carried her picture, every policeman was on the lookout, thousands of reports came in, to say that she had been seen or found; none was accurate.

"Check every movement she ever made," Roger said. "Try to find out if she's been seen in any particular district in the past. Try everything."

"You haven't forgotten Hann-Gorlay, have you?" Sloan asked.

"I'm going to se him," Roger said, "as soon as the doctors give the go-ahead."

Peel himself was checking Hann-Gorlay, going back over his movements, finding out just where he had been with Ruth.

Then a watchful patrolman remembered seeing Ruth and Prescott in the Surbiton area. Close questioning of other men supported this. They had been seen together, but Ruth and Prescott had been recognized in the district. The search was concentrated there.

240

The morning after Ruth's escape, Roger walked up the stairs leading to Brammer's flat. Brammer and Pauline had been released, after Lamb's statement; they were both here.

Pauline opened the door.

Brammer was just behind them, shaved, looking much fitter and brighter.

"Hallo," said Pauline, and her eyes were gay with welcome. "Any news?"

"Not yet."

"If you ask me," Brammer said, "Ruth is going to get away from you, Handsome. She'll have a comfortable spot ready in France or somewhere abroad."

"You sound almost as if you like the idea."

Brammer grinned twistedly.

"You know what I think about Ruth. But she is clever—you just have to admit that."

"She'll find that she can be too clever," Roger said. "You were right about Lamb and his wife, Pauline," he added. Then he turned back to Brammer. "Bram, you said you told Pauline that you suspected Lamb."

"Yes."

"Why? You weren't sure of Pauline, then—"

"That's why. I hadn't anything on Lamb, really —and I thought that if I told Pauline and then she warned Lamb, that would clinch the game as far as she was concerned. When I was shanghaied, I was pretty sure Pauline had passed on the news."

"Now you know she didn't."

"Of course she didn't!"

"Then why did they kidnap you?"

241

"They must have known I'd got on to Lamb some other way," said Brammer.

"That's the point—some other way. Yet if you only told Pauline—" Roger suddenly spun round. "Where did you tell her?"

"Where?" Brammer looked blank. "In my office. Why?"

"Could anyone have overheard you?"

"I don't think so—"

"Matthewson might have done," said Pauline very softly. "He was going in and out at the time. But he couldn't—"

"Couldn't he?" Roger breathed.

"Of course he couldn't!" Brammer exploded. "Damn it, he started the League. He wanted to form the vigilantes, to arm the police—"

"That's just it," said Roger tautly. "So did Ruth. Matthewson's the kind who could reason my way. He'd know that violence begets violence. Arm the police, and the tough boys arm themselves. The more vigilantes, the tougher the crooks. And Ruth has been seen in the Surbiton area—"

He broke off.

Suddenly Brammer grinned.

"You shouldn't have told us about this brainstorm, Handsome. We could warn him, couldn't we? Put us in the jug until you've been to see him."

"I'll trust you," Roger said thinly.

But he wondered whether he should, as he rushed back to the Yard to plan a visit to Matthewson.

Man-by-man interrogation at the Surbiton Police H.Q., followed by talks with milk roundsmen and other early risers, told that Matthewson's car

242

had come home in the early hours of the morning when Ruth had escaped.

Shopkeepers told of larger orders for food than usual, but no one had seen a visitor.

Sloan, Peel and a cordon were round Matthewson's house when Roger made his call.

Roger approached the front door briskly. It was late evening, and dark. A good night for coshmen and desperadoes.

He knew that Matthewson was home, but there was no way of being sure that Ruth was at the house, or that she had ever been there.

A maid answered, quite normally.

Roger waited in the hall while she went to tell Matthewson that he had called.

Matthewson came out of one room, closed the door firmly behind him, greeted Roger warmly, and led him into another room. He looked mild and benevolent, and his handshake was very firm.

"Very glad to see you, Chief Inspector. I've heard that Hann-Gorlay is much better—I'm delighted about that, delighted. And also really pleased—gratified—at the great success achieved by the police. I even dare hope that my own modest efforts stimulated you all a little."

He beamed.

"Nice of you," Roger said dryly. "I think you're going to stimulate us even more. Where's Ruth Linder?"

In that moment he knew that he was right. Matthewson was taken so completely by surprise that he couldn't speak, couldn't hide his consternation. He even glanced toward the door and the wall—as if trying desperately to warn Ruth.

243

Roger said gently, "So she's here. I—"

"West—no—you startled me! I don't understand—*West*—"

Roger drew his gun. In that moment he wanted to shoot. Matthewson simply swerved to one side and snatched at his pocket. Roger shot him in the arm, then leaped to the door and outside, slammed it, and turned the key in the lock. He went swiftly to the other, gun in hand.

It was locked.

He fired at the lock; the door sagged. He heard a window being thrust up as he pushed again. A police whistle blew; and a moment later he heard a shot from inside the room; another and another.

He put all his strength against the door, and it opened into the dining room. He staggered in. The light was on. The window leading to the back garden was open, and the wind blew in, stirring the curtains.

Ruth lay on the floor by the window, a gun close to her. There was a spreading crimson patch on her white blouse, near the left breast. Men were running from the garden, but she wasn't looking at them, she was looking at Roger.

He could tell that she was dying.

She moved her hand toward the gun, but the effort was too much for her. She touched but couldn't pick it up. She turned her lovely eyes toward him. The hatred that she bore for him and for the police shone in them—an evil light. Even as she was dying, the evil remained.

Sloan appeared at the window.

"Get a doctor," Roger said. "Hurry."

Ruth moistened her lips.

"He won't get here in time," she said. "You won't

244

be able to save my life so that you can hang me. I've fooled you, West, to the very end I've fooled you."

Ten minutes later, when a doctor arrived, she was dead.

An hour later, after the police had finished searching Matthewson's house, they found that as far back as the days of Uncle Benny's greatest prosperity, Matthewson had been buying and selling selected stolen jewels. Uncle Benny had always given him first choice among "hot" gems. Ruth had got to know Matthewson then, had been his mistress for years.

Matthewson cracked as easily as Lamb.

He was in love with Ruth. He loved her even more than wealth, which was saying plenty. His ambition was to win her love for him, and he was prepared to do anything to succeed. Matthewson also fed her hatred for the police, and used her vendetta to become the most powerful fence in the country. He had planned it all, from the beginning, and was worth a fortune. And Ruth, out of her hatred, had carried out all he had asked of her. He had worked on the emotions and wildness of youths with a vicious streak. Ruth had first infatuated them, then gradually brought them into the criminal orbit. Whenever she went on her errands to the smaller fences, she had two cosh-boys with her—to deal with any fence who argued.

Ruth was the only one who knew Matthewson's part in all this.

It had been Matthewson's idea to start the Citizens' League. He had reasoned in exactly the same way as Roger—violence would beget violence;

harsher punishments, arms for the police; vigilantes would put venom into the youths who were fighting the police. When he first told Ruth the idea, she was doubtful; but he converted her.

The League had to have a leader—a man of good name, an able speaker, an influential public figure. Matthewson approached Hann-Gorlay, and won him over—and introduced him to Ruth. And Ruth came nearer to loving a man than she had ever been in her life....

Too late Matthewson realized what had happened. Hann-Gorlay had become not only the acknowledged leader of the League, but had won Ruth.

At the Albert Hall meeting Matthewson saw how he might rid himself of Hann-Gorlay. The shooting was not arranged by him, he did not know the boy who had tried to kill Hann-Gorlay on the platform.

"A fanatic," he murmured to Roger, unconscious of the irony of the word. "But he gave me the idea. Hann-Gorlay was an obvious target for men of that sort. If another attack took place, not even Scotland Yard would look far for a motive. So I spoke to Mortimer and Gedd.

"I knew Mortimer was fond of Pauline Weston, but I didn't know he was infatuated with her. He knew that Ruth was trying to frame her. So when I put the proposition of killing Hann-Gorlay, by telephone, and sent him a lump payment in advance, he elaborated the idea without my knowledge.

"He planted stolen jewels, to frame Ruth.

"Not being able to help her then was a great grief to me," said Matthewson. He still looked dapper and self-possessed; was almost naïve. "Nothing, of course, to my grief now—"

Roger controlled himself with an effort. "What about the attacks on you yourself and the other League leaders?"

"They were to be expected," said Matthewson calmly. "Although we spread the word to those we could trust that the League should be left alone, we could hardly tell the whole of London's underworld that the League was really on their side, could we? There were bound to be some thugs"—he used the word contemptuously—"who would see us as enemies, and try to kill us. It was a risk that had to be taken. There was no need for Ruth herself to take that risk," he added. "I never wanted her to appear on the League platform. I kept her off at first, but Hann-Gorlay..."

"You would risk your life for her, and she would risk hers for him, eh?" Roger said.

The rest of Matthewson's story confirmed Lamb's. Matthewson added a few details that would help in the roundup of the gang, but little fresh general information.

"We nearly succeeded," he said regretfully. "At least, we nearly succeeded in getting an issue of arms for your people, didn't we?"

Roger said stonily, "That's your guess. Why did you release Brammer and me?"

"You, because Ruth was so anxious to make you look foolish," Matthewson said. "Brammer, because he was doing a most useful job for us through the *Courier* and the League. He had not got very far—he wasn't really dangerous until he got onto Lamb, and then he had to be removed. I arranged that with real regret, for he believed in the League and all it stood for, and was an ardent advocate."

247

"A devil's advocate," Roger said, under his breath.

With Sloan and Peel, he interviewed youth after youth during the next few days. Over fifty had been arrested, with five more leaders and suppliers of arms. Almost without exception they admitted to planning to carry weapons all the time if the vigilantes had been organized. Some, of the insolent type like Gedd, bragged that they had been longing for the day to dawn.

"Okay, Roger," Sloan said, when the interviewing was over. "I give you best. It still doesn't make sense to me, but I should say you're right."

Brammer, with his arm round Pauline, gave his familiar crooked grin. He looked better—less tired, and with a clearer complexion. His eyes were still bright but did not seem so heavily lidded.

They were in his flat.

"All right, Handsome," he said. "You've made out your case, and I lost mine. That doesn't mean I have to agree with you. In fact I don't—in spite of what Matthewson and the kids say. I say the only way to smack 'em down is by strong-arm methods. But I won't say so in the *Courier* for a while. I *will* try to get you new recruits."

"Just remember we don't want vigilantes," Roger said dryly.

"He'll remember," Pauline promised. "I'll see to that."

"Think it's really over?" Brammer asked.

"Oh, this show is," Roger said. "There'll be another surge of violence one of these days; more young fools will turn desperadoes, and there won't be enough police to cope. But there'll be a breathing space. I'll be able to see my wife and family occasionally. I might even get time off to attend a wedding, if I get plenty of notice."

"Next week," Brammer said. "It's fixed." His arm tightened round Pauline. "Otherwise she might start playing copper again, and we'd hate that."

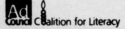